Praise for Past Secret Present Danger

"A fascinating novel weaving historical fact with fiction in a compelling tale of mystery, adventure, family ties and relationships between generations. The enthralling plot is easy to follow and the outcome unexpected, as the characters discover innovative ways to unearth the truth. From teens to seniors, this is a book everyone will enjoy. Captivating twists and turns keep the reader completely absorbed from the opening page until the end."

—Sue Augustine
Best-selling author of several books, including
"When Your Past is Hurting Your Present"

"Intrigue, suspense and an unknown family past all unfold in beautiful Niagara Falls... Margarete Ledwez's intimate relationship with both the area and characters bring the story to life for the reader and her gifted and clever writing will leave you longing for this book to become a series."

— Nerissa L.

"Margarete Ledwez has created a wonderful cast of highly believable and curious characters for this gripping story set in the tunnels under Niagara Falls. "Past Secret – Present Danger" makes for fascinating reading!"

—Ted Beaudoin, author of "Pilot of Fortune."

To David
enjoy!
Margarete Ledwez

Praise for Past Secret Present Danger

[illegible]

—Sue Augustine
Award-winning author of several books, including
"When Your Past Is Hurting Your Present"

[illegible]

—Norissa L.

[illegible]

—Ted Bensdorp, author of "Thief of Fortune"

Margarete Ledwez

ISBN 978-1-943492-32-9 (hard back)
ISBN 978-1-943492-31-2 (soft cover)

Book and cover design by **designpanache**.

All my grandchildren are precious to me, but I dedicate this book to one of them in particular–Josh.

His hard work paid off. He became an honor student.

During his journey he was reading a series of books and I joined him in the reading project. As he finished one book, I would read it. Josh couldn't put the books down and finished each one quickly. I couldn't wait to get my hands on them. I enjoyed seeing Josh entranced by the stories so much, I decided I would create a story that would capture both adult and teen.

Thank you for inspiring me, Josh.
Love, Oma.

Contents

Preface

In this book I am delighted to portray a network of real tunnels, once used but now long forgotten. The Queenston Chippawa Hydro Electric Plant was built in 1922 as the first large scale generating station in the world and featured 22-kilometer tunnels and cable tunnels, though many are now closed for safety reasons. (Video of persons entering and investigating the old systems can be found on the internet).

As a child, between the ages of 4 and 7 years, I lived in St. Catharines on Yates St. East, learning of tunnels right in our own back yard! It was the *Oak Hill, William Hamilton Merritt Estate* (currently home to a radio station, CKTB) and there are three tunnels. Two lead down to the *Twelve Mile Creek* below and one to the carriage house, sadly no longer there. They were used to hide slaves via the *Underground Railroad* and used by bootleggers during the Prohibition days. In 1967 they were sealed for safety reasons.

St. Catharines proved to have a variety of tunnels. *The Blue Ghost Tunnel* was a favorite area for snowmobiling in winter. It was located behind the GM plant in St. Catharines, but very accessible from our home near the Falls

We stumbled upon the tunnels at the *Dolls' House Gallery* quite by accident. In the days before the internet, my daughters were interested in expanding the furnishings for their miniature dollhouse, so we went to see the *Mildred M. Mahoney Dolls' House Gallery* on the banks of the Niagara River in Fort Erie. While there we became intrigued by stories of tunnels. They too were boarded up for safety's sake.

The *Macklem House* was built in the 1850s by Thomas Clark Macklem, at the intersection of Main St. and the Niagara River Parkway in Chippawa. It burned down in 1930, but not before rumors of tunnels from the house to the riverbank emerged.

We took outings to the tunnels at *Fort George* and *Fort Mississauga*, and even as we traveled we would stop at underground caverns to discover the beauty beneath the minimal façade. Our curiosity grew and was cultivated, as we never knew what lay around the next corner.

When I began writing this book I drew from the unending intrigue that there could very well be many more tunnels that have never been discovered. I was speaking to someone not long ago who saw two tunnel entrances beneath the *Riverbend Inn.* They are also boarded up for the safety of those, like me, who are too curious!

So, while this book is a work of fiction, many of the landmarks are authentic. Some of the names portray real people while others are invented or purely coincidental.

ML

Characters

Angelica—*Mark's mom*

Barry— *Mac's dad, police officer and family friend*

Bee—*Brianna, Josh's sister*

Carly—*Bee's friend and co-worker*

Dad—*Josh's father*

Dr. Gerard—*associate of John Schultz*

Grammy—*Josh's Grandmother on his mom's side*

Grammpy—*Josh's Grandfather on his mom's side*

Jake—*a family friend with Amish connections*

John Schultz—*doctor and friend*

Josh—*main character, 15 years old*

Kelly—*friend of Grammy, used to be Amish*

Landlord—*the original owner of the mansion property*

Mac—*Josh's life-long friend, a 15-year-old girl*

The Suit—*man in car at hospital*

Mark—*Josh's friend, also 15*

Mom—*Nerissa, "Nissa", Josh's mom*

Mr. Stolzfus—*the Amish driver*

Opa Wittfoot—*Josh's Great-Grandfather*

Oma Wittfoot—*Josh's Great-Grandmother*

Omz—*Josh's Grandmother on his dad's side*

Pa—*Josh's Grandfather on his dad's side*

Vinnie—*Angelica's supposed relative*

Witness—*saw Bee's accident*

CHAPTER 1

The Old Mansion

The house had a moonlit glow with all the uncovered windows.

Slowly and quietly I crept past my mother's bedroom door. Making no sound, I tightly but carefully clutched my exploring pouch. My tall slender frame was tense from trying to keep every muscle in control. I finally arrived at the back door. A few more steps and I would find freedom once again.

As I stood tall and stretched I realized just how much my body was strained over trying to become invisible. Now 15, I had grown to be tall and not accustomed to my new stature. One thing I did know was that I could take care of myself. Being the youngest my parents thought I still needed supervision. I would prove them wrong. My blonde wavy hair and blue eyes accompanied with that clear complexion gave me a young baby face appearance, not measuring up to the maturity level for my age. My quiet nature disguised the fact that I was confident and knew what direction I needed to take in the immediate future. Concentrating once again, I slowly let go of my noisy pouch, now hanging freely from my belt, only to grasp it again as its contents rattled.

The door closed quietly as I held it tightly and pulled it. We never locked our doors, as this was a safe and friendly neighbourhood. I never used a key although one was hidden near by. As I looked back at the old coach house, that I now called home, I tried to discipline my mind to refocus on the mansion. The old house lay deserted in the direction my feet were moving but my mind could not leave the carriage house and the safety that lay within.

Everyone I loved was back there in that house except for Dad and Pa. I remembered how Pa had loved the old carriages, and how he cared and spoke of them as if to regain his youth. I loved that man I called Pa. Ever since I was very young he gave me insight into so many facets of life. He also left me with numerous questions regarding the same.

I needed to focus on the task ahead. The aged mansion soon to be demolished, had unanswered questions, introduced to me by my pa. Tonight I would try to solve some of these. When I got into the house it was like being with an old friend. I ran those halls so many times and investigated those rooms, with my senior family friend. I listened to all those magnificent stories that accompanied our steps.

Again distracted, I thought of Dad travelling to so many places near and far in search of clues to Pa's disappearance. Dad was almost a carbon copy of my Pa only shorter. He thought he should be able to think like him and discover his secrets as well as his whereabouts.

Tonight, it would be just Mac and me. Mac knew this place, almost as well as I did. She would often meet me here in our secret hiding place. Mackenzie was a family friend who became known as Mac to all who knew her well.

Her sense of adventure was equal to mine and we enjoyed each other's company. The old mansion stood near the edge of the gorge surrounded by native trees and fauna. Beyond the crest of the gorge the mighty Niagara River flowed at the bottom of the high cliffs of grey rock. Pa told me of a secret cave entrance, somewhere down there. That knowledge was our secret, Pa's and mine, although I never saw it myself. With determination, I was going to find it one day. If my Grandfather saw it, I would too!

The mansion was nicely placed on the back of this property and the wide porches around its perimeter made it look stately. I took out my flashlight and quickly looked around. The moonlight was so bright that I didn't need my light, but rather held it tightly for security. Entering the side French doors, facing the ravine and the gazebo, I stopped in my tracks, realizing for the first time that this entrance was the one I always used, my favorite.

Pa repeatedly told me that every room had two exits. We knew of only one room, with a secret passage! I headed towards the far wall of the room and stood in front of the secret panel. Leaning just a little to the left of the panel, it pushed in.

I heard a scream! It was Mac of course.

Quickly I commanded Mac to be quiet and not give us away.

"Who did you expect, Jack the Ripper?" was my response.

Mac laughed under her breath.

"Well what are we looking for today?" was her next response.

I shone my flashlight at her face noticing her long brown curly hair in a tousled ponytail and her appealing freckles.

We were in a small inside hall with no windows. Only the two of us knew about it, or so we thought. Mac had always been much taller than me, but in the last couple of years my stature has become equal if not more than hers. Our relationship was one in which height had no consequence. We were life-long friends.

"Get that out of my eyes!" demanded Mac.

I spoke softly," I think we should try to find Pa's secret passage from his study."

The wall that opened should have taken us directly to the study but led us into a small hall. This did not make sense. There was a space between the study wall and the family room wall, where we just came from.

We carefully felt our way along the hideaway walls, looking at every detail with our flashlight. It looked ordinary and smelled of old lumber and dust. We had hidden in here many times as children to escape from family.

"Ouch!" Mac caught herself on a protruding nail.

We had played in here so many times and were never tall enough to be near this nail.

As my flashlight flooded her I said, "What's the matter?"

"It's this nail," she muttered while tearing herself loose.

As she tugged on her jacket, a piece of board came out from the wall, and hung, slightly turned sideways. We were shocked as the floor gave way!

We slid down a wooden ramp to who knew where.

Pa was right, there was more to this place than anyone realized. I clutched my flashlight as if my life depended on it. We twisted and turned until we came to a sudden halt, ending up like two sacks of stacked grain. It took a few seconds to realize what happened.

"We did it! We did it!" I said. We found another one. But… this was not Pa's study. We were down below somewhere.

"Wow, now what should we do?"

I shone my light up the shaft from where we came, and to my surprise, it looked like a long way up. We hoped the trap door had not closed behind us, as it was too dark to tell; and the shaft curved so many times.

CHAPTER 2

New Discoveries

The flashlight lit the area, and we could see a nicely appointed storage room with tidy shelves directly in front, across from the ramp. They were stocked with canned goods, tools, and rolled up plans. This was only at first glance.

As we investigated some more, Mac said, "Hey.... macaroni and cheese! Someone must have been down here within the last few years!"

There were sealed containers of oatmeal, rice, cookies, dried fruit, and more, all repackaged so as not to let moisture in.

The cool dampness overtook our bodies. Mac was wrapping her arms around herself for heat as I had put my hands in my pocket. As excited as I was it gave me an eerie feeling to be down here in the darkness.

Mac repeated, "Look at this; someone was planning on an extended stay down here."

While nodding my head, I looked at one of the maps. It was a newer one and had the main house drawn on it. Not too intrigued, I looked for another. My eyes caught sight of an old print, but it made no sense to me as I stared it.

Lines were drawn to the cliffs, to the edge of the gorge. What was that all about? I didn't know about any fault lines in our area!

Were we in danger? was my first thought.

No, we hadn't felt an earthquake here—ever—or for as long as

I could remember.

Pa never told me about one either. He lived here most of his life, except for the investigative trips to far-off lands of course. The trips only lasted a few months at a time I thought, recalling the loneliness and boredom in his absence.

Mac jolted me back to reality by pulling on my arm.

"Where are we, do you know?"

"No", I squeaked out unexpectedly.

"Oh, okay," she said.

"We will take stock of what we have. We are not hurt, right?"

"Right," she replied.

"We have lots of food and other supplies. We need water, and, is there a place to cook all these supplies?" I added.

We shone the light around and our eyes landed on an old lantern already filled with kerosene.

"There must be some matches somewhere."

"Oh, up there, on the second shelf! There are so many."

As we lit the dusty aged specimen, it gave our eyes relief from their strain. We had a look around, taking in our new surroundings. It felt much cozier with the light on and it would have made a nice hideout.

"Now is there water? Whoever stocked this place must have thought about water, they supplied everything else," Mac spoke quietly while examining cans of food.

There were also old tin cans filled with nails, and screws. The slide came down in the middle of the room. Large wooden crates neatly positioned, made two long benches on the left side of the slide facing the room. To the right of the slide were two old wooden barrels, one labeled GUN POWDER. We looked in the other since it had no label and found it empty. That seemed odd, as the detail to function and purpose of the materials in this room, were as if calculated. An empty barrel just didn't make sense.

As one crate lid was carefully lifted, Mac sighed, "Does this mean we are stuck here, for a long time?"

"No!" I replied finding a sleeping bag, pillow and a blanket in the box. They were expecting one person not two. The other crate had writing material, paper, pencils and even an old typewriter. It looked familiar but I couldn't place it at that moment.

We anxiously opened the next one and found an old Coleman stove, as well as a small frying pan, pot and some utensils. The crates were far from full but their contents were tidy besides being very useful.

"Boy, someone was thorough."

What was in the last crate? They were all two and a half feet high and wide, as well as four feet long. They reminded me of the kind of crates people used for travel in the days my Pa was young. In the days when he and his parents moved from Germany, most people travelled with their precious belongings in the large, sturdy, homemade wooden boxes. I heard many stories of these crates and how precious they were. This one had writing on one side—*Deutschland zu Kanada*. The letters were hand painted in a bold script. It was nailed shut, not like the others. We looked for a tool that we could use to pry the lid. Nothing worked! Wow this was such a secured piece of wood and a difficult task. It almost seemed to be attached from the bottom under the lid.

Mac said, "Let's see if there is a way out. I'm not sure how long we can last down here, nor do I want to."

She was getting a little antsy about being underground and not knowing how to get out.

To reassure her I said, "Pa said every room has two exits. One is a very long slide and the other...?"

My eyes carefully scanned the room with new determination. I started by tapping the walls and listening for anything different. It all sounded the same.

What now?

We decided to sit down and catch our breath as we discussed our options. Could we climb back up the long slide and open the trap door from the bottom? I tried to move my body up the slide as if I was going somewhere. The waxy finish on the wood was so polished that I just could not stay up, and kept sliding back down. I took a run at it and clutched to the sides with my fingers. After much effort, I said we would need a rope from the top all the way down to get out this way. Mac was getting a worried look on her face so I suggested we try some of the food.

Mac said, "Mac 'n' Cheese…sounds good to me."

I reminded her that we did not have any water.

And I also reminded her of our secret password and what it meant if we ever needed it to prove our identity to each other.

She said yes she remembered and how could she forget.

We opened a can of peas and I came to a quick realization. There was enough liquid in the can to quench our thirst, or make us sick.

"Oh, Yuck, that is terrible Josh, but I guess it will have to do."

The crackers were stale so we opened a can of pork and beans to finish our meal. I told Mac that, although we didn't say grace before we ate I was very grateful for the food we found down here. She agreed.

Our investigation of this peculiar space had made time fly in a way that I had never experienced before. No wonder we were hungry. My watch said it was very early in the morning. We had been here all night and soon our parents would miss us for breakfast. We had to get back.

I would use one of the crates for spreading out some plans. The wooden barrel would make a great seat if I could pull it over. We could spread them out on the oversized boxes as we scoured for a way out.

The barrel seemed heavy even though it was empty. I used my body to try to pick it up. With a big hug and using every ounce of strength, it moved. I turned it counter-clockwise instead of picking it up. It turned so easily but why wouldn't it lift off its base?

Mac screamed.

Suddenly the crate beside her on the opposite side of the room moved towards the wooden slide, revealing a large hole in the stone floor.

"What is it?" I asked as I ran over.

What was in there?

I grabbed my flashlight and my protective instinct kicked in as I motioned for Mac to stay back. Hopeful of finding a way out, I shone the light into the opening, only to find someone peering back at me.

I found a reflection of myself in a pool of water. I could see myself! It was water all right. It looked like a natural spring. I know Pa said his parents had no running water in the early days, but used spring water that tasted better than anything he had ever tasted.

"Give me a scooper and let's try some."

Without thinking, Mac handed me the ladle and I reached down and retrieved some. We thought it looked clean, but would it taste good? While I raised the water to my lips, Mac decided to let her emotions show. She started to cry and sob aloud. I stopped as my brow furrowed and fear took over my mind for the first time.

"What's the matter?" I almost shouted.

"You might die," she said in between sobs. "What would I do?"

"Okay, okay, we will not taste it until later. We will try to get out first."

"Oh, I don't want to be down here alone," she said as the sobbing slowly stopped. "Can you close that, it scares me."

In all the years I 'd known her, I had never seen Mac like this before.

CHAPTER 3

The Other Exit

My eyes were directed over to the other side of the slide. The barrels stood side by side. I walked over to hug the one in the corner again. My intention was to move the crate back over the water hole, by manipulating the barrel once again. Clumsily, I tripped and fell against the barrel. In the turned position, it tipped over so easily. I fell forward and ended up lying on it. Hoping I didn't break the mechanism that controlled the crate, protecting the pool of water, I opened my eyes. They immediately looked over to the crate, in the direction of Mac. She looked frozen and horrified, her jaw dropped as she stared in my direction.

"What? It's not so bad!" I retorted figuring I didn't break anything.

She pointed, with an outstretched arm, her face still in that spaced-out state!

I turned, not knowing what to expect. There was an opening in the wall behind me.

Yes, another exit!

"We did it!" A smile took over my face.

I asked Mac to bring the lantern and I grabbed my flashlight again. Mac was so close behind me I could feel her breathe down my neck. I didn't blame her; it must have been haunting to see that wall opening behind me.

The movies would have had a monster appear now.

Our minds only thought of one direction, and that was up. With my light shining upwards, we focused on a narrow rustic rock stairway leading upward. To where, we didn't know, but it was up. We knew we needed to go in the upward direction, and that was all we cared about.

I stopped in my tracks, before leaving the room.

"Oh, Mac let's take a small container of water with us."

"Okay," she answered me.

As she went to get a small sample, I scanned the room to make sure everything was as it was found. The plans had been put back on the shelves, and all was clean and put away.

I put the sample into my exploration pouch. It hung on my hip, making noise as usual.

"Do you think we should leave the lantern here?" Mac questioned.

"I think this time we will take it, and when we come back again, we will return it to its designated place.

"Okay, you hold the flashlight, Mac, I will carry the lantern and go ahead of you."

She stayed close as we moved forward slowly, one step at a time. We didn't even wonder if the door would close or stay open, we just needed to get back home.

"I wonder how many steps there are?" I mused while shining the light on my watch. We were climbing for at least fifteen minutes. Our pace was slow and cautious but this was ridiculous. We should be somewhere by now. The steps were irregular and there were large rocks that jutted out on the sides. The narrow tunneled passage wound around and turned as it twisted its way upward.

Finally we arrived and saw a glimmer of daylight ahead in the shape of a line. The tunnel opened. We hurried and found ourselves in an old, round, wood structure. It was high enough to stand in and had a wooden flat ceiling. We came up inside it.

As I peeked through a crack in the weathered wood planks, I muttered, "Hey, we are under the old gazebo."

It hadn't been used in many, many years, as the old structure needed of a lot of repair. My friends and I used it, often against my parent's wishes. Although I must say they did not forbid it. They figured it wasn't the safest place to hang out. It stood unusually high as to get the best view of the gorge and river below. This was the best place to catch the evening breezes on those warm summer nights.

We quietly snuck onto its refuge many times as we finished playing "Hide and Go Seek" or "Marco Polo." Always on the gazebo of course, and not underneath where we were now.

"Now how do we get out, without alarming anyone else, and giving ourselves away?"

We put the lantern out quickly and left it near the circular wood wall for another time. I took my flashlight and studied the interior boards.

Where was the exit?

To our left, I spotted a light switch. We couldn't find the light fixture but decided that I would pull it and see what happened.

"Here it goes," I said and pulled.

Suddenly, from somewhere in the tunnel, we could see an ever so slight glow and faint shadows against the hard rock walls. There was light down there. Next time we would make use of it. For now, I just turned it off.

My eyes weren't more than a foot past the light switch when I spotted a latch on the wall. It was at the back of the gazebo on the cliff side. If I remembered correctly, erosion had taken the bank up to the backside of the old structure. I hoped not, but we had to try it. We focused on the latch, and found the section of boards that made a door.

The old plank escape was easily opened. My heart was pounding as I slowly cracked open the door. Mac drew a huge breath. It was far too close to the edge of the gorge. I would have to find another way out. There was no room to get out on that side.

Closing the door, I thought to myself, "Someone could fall and be killed leaving from here."

I decided to use my pocketknife and pull off some of the old wide boards from the structure. Between the gorge and the high outside stairs was a good place, and no one would see us come and go.

The stairs led up eight feet to the stately looking gazebo. Its Victorian trim, although weather beaten, was still intact. Besides offering a magnificent view, it charmed anyone who gazed upon it.

Our exit would be unnoticed, especially if we put the boards back afterwards. The stairs made a natural camouflage between us, and any point on the rest of the property. The stairs led down to the ravine, which ran along the whole side of our property. It was rarely used by anyone. No one but my friends and I, that is.

With the wide old boards worked loose we squeezed out.

Crouched down behind the stairs, we got our story straight. If our parents caught us we would say we were jogging this morning. Hopefully no one would see us coming from the old gazebo. The cycling path along the river road was the best for jogging. We should be coming from that direction. We just better not get caught.

We also made plans to get some shuteye and meet here tonight at dinner time. We would pretend to sleep at our friend's houses, Mac at hers, and me at Mark's.

In fact, I thought to myself, Mark would enjoy this adventure as much as the two of us.

"See you tonight," I whispered.

"And don't forget to test the water!" Mac added.

"I won't, Mac, see ya."

CHAPTER 4

Dad's Return

I crept back into the house quiet as a mouse. The soft sound of Mom's voice humming was competing with the sound of the water of the shower. I was successful at sneaking back in. Bee would be sleeping in for sure. My door closed gently and I was back, no one the wiser. Hopefully Mac had the same luck as I did. Quickly I dropped my clothes on the floor, stepping out of them and crawled into bed although my thoughts were wild and erratic.

"Did we really find that room and the secret passages? I know we did, but who built them and what else would we discover?"

I finally must have dozed off, when a noise roused my senses. I woke with a jolt. It was Mom calling my name.

"What," I yelled, "I'm sleeping."

Mom bolted through the door, "Are you alright?"

She felt my forehead. She knew I never slept in and would rather get up early to play my games on our new TV. After all, I wasn't seventeen like my sister, who loved sleeping in with a passion.

"Did you forget that your father is coming home today and we are picking him up from the Buffalo Airport?"

Jumping up with a jolt I had little time to feel tired. My shower took only minutes, and I was ready before Bee. I had called her that since I could utter my first word and it seemed to stick as her nickname.

Dad had been away for months and it was going to be great for all of us to have him back. He went to finish some project that Pa had started, before he disappeared.

"How does that happen in this day and age with all of our technology?" My Pa disappeared!

Dad put all of our money into trying to find out what happened to Pa, and we still have no idea of his circumstances. There was no trace of Pa, anywhere. Pa knew the secrets of the old mansion and had hinted at some of them to me.

Did Dad know? I had so many questions!

I would try to get some information without tipping anyone off to what we had found.

I decided to start with Mom and asked exactly what it was that Dad did. She was evasive as usual and said he was taking over my pa's business.

"You know he took over his dad's business, of investigating."

Was that what they expected me to do? How did I know if I would like that career? They won't even tell me details about it.

"What do your qualifications have to be anyways?"

Mom laughed as Bee looked up from her smart phone to see what was so funny.

"I think you have more than your share, but don't know it yet, Josh. Give it time."

I just sat back and thought about my secret room and all the neat contraptions, the slide, the exposed water pool and the wall panel that moved. I had to find out what they were for, and of course, who used them. For the rest of our trip I sat still as a mouse, mulling over and over all those new details Mac and I had discovered.

When we saw Dad at the airport, he looked a little tired, and had lost some weight. He had a bronze tan, contrasting his fair, not so apparent hair. We enjoyed having his strong arms around us again as he engaged us with his huge bear hug. That was one thing I missed about Pa too, he and Dad gave the best bear hugs ever.

I tried to pry some information out of Dad, but I could tell he just wanted to catch up and hear about home and what he had missed. I could have told him some great news, but I didn't know enough yet.

Maybe after tonight we would know more.

For now, it was nice to be a family again, and I enjoyed seeing Mom happy, with her cheerful smile.

I knew they would go to sleep early tonight, as Dad was yawning frequently. He said the time change was getting to him. Around five-thirty Mom and Dad retreated to their room as they were worn out, and gave in to the emotions of the day. It seemed to me they were not telling us everything and needed to have a private talk.

Bee and I cleaned up the dishes and put the delicious leftovers in the fridge. Mom had cooked Dad's favorite meal of course and we almost made gluttons of ourselves.

Bee drove herself to work at the Lodge, accompanied by Carly, a friend who also worked with her.

I was anxious to get going. In my pouch, I packed an extra mini flashlight. I had put the water sample in a dish for the cat before we left for the airport. She was one of my favorite pets and I loved the 8 years we spent together. The water was gone and the cat was still alive. It proved the water was good.

"Mac will be so relieved," I mused.

There was no sneaking out as I was supposed to be walking to my friend Mark's place, not far from our home. He lived just across the road from Mac's place, on the side of our property where the small cemetery lay.

I sat crouched, out of sight, behind the gazebo stairs, which hid the entrance to the tunnel below.

Leaning against the old boards, I sensed an odd presence. It was still a few minutes to our set meeting time, so I sat listening to the birds high in the trees doing their daily visitation. The wind was calm as I listened for the sound of footsteps.

I enjoyed our summer holidays and all that went with them. The varieties of flowers and the fragrances of freshly cut grass were my top two. Since Dad was away much of the time, it was my job to do the outdoor chores.

The time I spent investigating the ravine that ran down the side of Pa's property filled in the rest of my hours. One section of the old stone-stacked wall surrounding the property was near to where I was sitting.

You could see how much skill it took to build it as it had stood the test of time and could still be enjoyed today. Students of early architecture were actually learning how to build this kind of stone-stacked wall at Willow Bank.

The gazebo was built near the top of the slope, which the ravine created. One side of the gazebo foundation was underground and the part on the ravine was exposed. The stairs led down onto an unkempt path. It was lined with shrubs and a variety of self-sustaining perennials. The shrubs were overgrown. I wondered why Pa never wanted to restore the gazebo to its former glory. He preferred to leave it just as it was, looking quite natural.

In our leisure time, we enjoyed this beautiful area along the Niagara River. We made memories walking the tourist-lined streets of Niagara-on-the-Lake. People dodged in and out of the historic buildings. The park was one of our favorite places in the old town. We hung out and met friends, and often went home soaked from being pushed into the park's shallow wading pool.

The old clock tower was interesting too, holding me captive with its intrigue. Pa told me it too had a secret. When would I find the answer to some of these secrets? My mind just wandered from one place to another.

I was suddenly startled by a "Boo!"

My body quaked from the pit of my stomach and I threw myself forward. Looking behind me, I could see the boards moving and Mac's hands waving for me to hurry. She had been hiding under the gazebo because she was early, and had replaced the boards so I would not suspect her being there.

"You sure jumped," she quietly laughed.

"You would too if it was you," I replied.

She was in a hurry to go down the tunnel stairs and do some investigating.

"Let's go," Mac said, "and you first."

I grabbed the lantern and quickly lit it with the lighter from my pouch. It was still quite dark so we each took one of my two flashlights. The stairs were cut out of grey, black rock and wound and turned even more than we remembered. Something seemed different!

What was it?

The dim light had barely illuminated our footsteps and after a while we realized it was taking us much longer than before. It seemed like our direction had changed. Was it my imagination? I remembered my compass. Pa said never to leave without one, and I had taken his advice. Reaching into my bag, I dug around until I found it.

My hunch was right. We were traveling towards the gorge, and not towards the old mansion. I kept my compass in my hand and watched as we descended. Then there was a straight stretch of stairway. We knew we were in new territory.

We had been going down the stairs for a long time. I knew it was because we were so cautious and taking our time, but we were both becoming concerned.

Was there no end to this, and why had we missed our secret room?

Mac suggested we sit down and take a break. She was tired of carrying the lantern and wondered if we should turn back rather than continue. We sat on the cold rock step, as the dampness made us shiver, and looked at each other. We could feel a chill now that we had stopped moving. Since there had been no light for quite some time, the two flashlights came in handy. Mac shone her light at me as I was scanning the frigid walls with mine. She looked worried again.

While I was wondering if she was still with me in this, she said, "Well we had better keep going."

I tilted my baseball cap and nodded as I spoke,

"Let's leave the lantern here and pick it up on the way back, okay?"

Mac inquired, "Do you think this takes us right to the bottom of the gorge?"

"I don't know, and if it does, I am curious to know why," I muttered.

We could feel a slight cold draft. It sent a chill down my spine and I shook. It got colder and draftier as we went into the bowels of the earth. Our legs were getting weary as we travelled further and further. I am sure it was a result of the tension we were feeling.

Suddenly, we saw a motionless black silhouette up ahead. We couldn't make out what it was. Getting closer it seemed like a huge black hole. No rock, no steps, no nothing. We stopped, sensing danger.

I motioned for Mac to be still and put her light off.

Cautiously I let my light fall upon the darkness.

There was a massive jagged opening, which I figured was about 30 feet high by 10 feet wide. My eyes tried to focus and see what was in there. I could only see rock formations and tall shadows as the light passed over. The stairs ended here. Should we enter or turn back?

CHAPTER 5

The Black Hole

Looking into the darkness ahead, I could see a faint, misty aura of light. I shone my flashlight up high, and Mac did the same. It looked like a crevasse in the rock with a small opening to the outside. The moon beamed a foggy stream of light through the natural opening, into the otherwise dark cavern. We had to go further, but first I would check our direction with my compass. We were going directly south, not knowing where we would end up.

"Mac, we have to go north, to return to this point, okay?"

"Got it."

With our lights shining on the ground ahead of us, we walked slowly. It was cold and damp and our bodies were cooling.

Doing up our jackets, with collars tightly wrapped around our necks, for both security and warmth, I told Mac to stay close. She nodded intently, as she stepped on my heel.

"Hey, not that . . .close!"

With a deep breath, she replied in agreement.

It seemed as though we weren't descending, but still stepping through tricky-to-navigate areas that were slippery and wet. Moving cautiously not wanting to fall, we came to a junction.

The obviously human-made tunnel lay right in front, crossing our path.

"Do you have a preference on the scenery, Mac?" I asked

"Let's go left," she replied

"Okay then we will have to remember how to get back."

"Next time we should bring a pencil and paper?"

"Always attention to detail, eh, Mac?"

It was an excellent idea, and we would make a point of it.

The tunnel was quite easy to travel but continued downwards at a comfortable slant.

There were very slight deviations from straight, but nothing dramatic. We thought we could see a hint of the moon's glow.

We got to an opening in the tunnel and realized we were back outside.

The night air filled our nostrils with a reminder of just how wonderful a summer night it was. It was a long way down from the top. The rock boulders jutted out above us and with the shrubs and trees made a nice protective covering. The drop to the bottom could kill a person. We had descended a fair distance but were surprised at how far we would have to go to get to the bottom of the gorge.

CHAPTER 6

At the End of the Tunnel

From this distance it was magnificent seeing the rapids glistening in the moonlight.

There was a magic that happened as the water made white foam, and moonbeams caused the rapids to dance in unison. We wished we could get closer to the water to investigate. Peering over the edge, as close as we could get, we saw it was too great a distance. It also looked too dangerous!

If we slipped, we could be smashed on the boulders or swept away by the raging current.

It was so tranquil our spirits embraced this place of quietude. We had forgotten how far we had come and just gazed as though in some hypnotic state. We sat there for quite some time and had no intension of moving.

Suddenly there was a loud, "WRRRRRRR!"

"What was that?" Mac blurted trying to whisper.

"It sounded like a cat, and not a small one at that. I hope it isn't hungry."

Suddenly, in the distance behind us we saw two eyes glaring like marbles in the night.

We knew we would have to hide, and started back into the tunnel. With our flashlights on, we ran until we got to the crossroads. The cougar might live in the black hole cavern, so we headed straight into the unexplored tunnel. We heard the cougar in the tunnel behind us.

Now what?

We were trapped.

We shone our light around, and spotted a little black hole in the rock. I peered in with my light. If we could get through the small opening we could hide for a while, or at least until the cougar left. It looked to be a small cave but would hold both of us.

"I will help you Mac. Come on, get in."

As I franticly pushed her body in she hit her head on a jagged rock and screamed.

We heard the growl again and this time closer. I squeezed in the opening just in time.

The huge animal lunged at the opening and its paw clawed at us.

I saw a large loose rock beside Mac and grabbed it. It took all my energy but my adrenaline was pumping, and I pulled the rock to the opening. The next attack, from our pursuer, came with force but the rock held its position. My feet were against it for extra support and peace of mind. We were safe from those claws, and ferocious jaws for a while. Without finding refuge in our newly found shelter, we would be at the mercy of our captor.

After I calmed down, I noticed Mac's head was bleeding.

She gave herself quite a gash and we needed to stop the loss of blood. In my bag, I carried a bandage, gauze and the smallest tube of Polysporin you ever saw. After putting pressure on the cut I assured her that it wasn't severe and told her that head wounds tend to bleed a lot. I dressed it and she felt much better except for the throbbing headache. I checked her pupils and it looked like she had a slight concussion.

I didn't tell her, as I knew that she would be terrified. I knew I would have to wake her up every hour throughout the night. At least I hoped it was every hour!

CHAPTER 7

A Long Night

I told Mac that we were safe and we would have to stay here until morning, so she should get comfortable. She moved around a little and I gave her my jacket to put her head on. I set my watch to go off on the hour, and was careful to use the vibration mode and not the audible alarm.

I did not want to scare her more than she was already. I was worried and that worst-case scenario, I would never be able to carry her up by myself. Would that cat still be waiting? I had my small pocketknife and, oh yes, that firecracker.

Did I still have my lighter in my bag? I checked to see. Yes I did. Sitting back in relief I sighed and felt my body relax a little. I could see my friend was relaxed and had her eyes closed. It frightened me a bit, but I told myself she would be fine.

As I was praying silently and thanking God for guiding us to this shelter, the cat made itself known once more. Of course, my senses became totally alert and guarded. It took until the next four times of waking Mac to be able to let myself relax again.

We spoke each time I woke Mac. We still had at least five hours before I felt safe enough to try to get out. I hoped Mac could climb the stairs in her condition. I almost dozed off just once—like that would have been possible—then I felt the vibration of my watch and almost jumped to my feet. I decided that from now on we would have to be more careful and better prepared.

I would have to bring my cell phone, an even warmer jacket and other emergency equipment. We should have brought that lantern all the way down with us. It would have provided us with warmth. Thank goodness the large black cave was easy walking, except for the slippery areas. We would have to be more careful. It was early in the morning. I thought it would be a safe to try for the exit. Mac was awake and seemed to feel good except for a slight headache.

CHAPTER 8

Journey Back

This was the plan. I would roll the rock away and we would wait for a while before climbing out, just in case our predator was still prowling close by. I would go first. Mac would be ready to push the rock back with her feet if something happened to me, or if I had to run for my life.

"Are you ready?" I asked.

She nodded her head, with a not so convincing gesture, and adjusted herself for anything. I rolled the rock towards Mac so she could push it with her feet, as the side of the cave would brace her body for strength. Exiting quietly, feet first, I just stood there. My flashlight was on as I waited. It was a long minute looking around in an unsettled fashion. I motioned for her to come out. When her feet hit the ground, she started to drop. I caught her and held her against the cold wall.

"Are you alright?"

Whispering, she said, "I think so but give me a second to adjust. I feel dizzy."

Agreeing, I supported her against the rock until she seemed to stand on her own.

Mac switched her flashlight on and we slowly made our way to the large black cave. When we came to the slippery rocks, I supported Mac, in case she fell and hit her head again. We made it to the stairs leading up.

We were taking too much time to reach the lantern; it would take forever to get to the top. Mac was getting weary and we stopped many times to rest. At one point I put her arm over my shoulder and almost dragged her.

I tied my flashlight to the top of my runner with my shoelace. I loosened my lace and stuck the flashlight under it before pulling and tying it tightly.

It left my hands free to support Mac. The lantern had been carefully wrapped in my jacket and attached to my belt. I positioned it at the back of my body so it wouldn't hit the rock walls and get smashed. It seemed like hours as we would take-a-few-steps-and-stop when she just couldn't go any further.

"I can't make it," she said with a weak voice.

Just sit here and rest," I answered. My mind was going a hundred miles an hour, should I leave her here and come back?

As if knowing what I was going to say, she said, "Please don't leave me alone down here!"

"Let me just go up a few steps and see if we are near the top, okay?"

"We haven't heard the cat today," I quickly added. Reluctantly she agreed, with a request.

"Can you put the lantern on?"

"Good idea!"

I carefully unwrapped it, and set it on the step above her. My lighter was handy and I lit the lantern. Even I enjoyed its warm glow and being able to see our surroundings so completely.

"Thanks."

"I won't be long. You will be able to hear me, okay?"

As I looked at her I could see her wound was bleeding heavily and soaking her bandages.

There was no time to lose.

One flashlight was still tied to my shoe and the other in my hand. I made my way up the stairs. The flashlight in my hand slipped and hit the rock floor. It went out, and I thought it had broken. Bending over to retrieve it I hit something with my right arm, and it moved.

I stood up just in time to see the rock wall slide open. It was our secret storage room. I dared not enter in case Mac and I got separated. I couldn't leave her any longer than I needed. I put the broken flashlight on the step, in front of the open room, and headed back. It would be a marker in case the door closed. It wasn't far now, and maybe she could make it.

"I found the room!" I half shouted as I neared the lantern.

"Mac, where are you?" Where would she have gone?

My heart was pounding against my chest cavity and I thought it would jump right out.

Running past the lantern and rounding the corner I saw her in a slumped mound.

"Mac, are you okay?"

There was no response.

"Mac, Mac!" I almost yelled as I grabbed both her shoulders.

As she slowly tried to lift her head in my direction she mumbled something.

"What, what did you say?"

She tried again and I understood: "I tried to get out, then I felt light headed."

"But you went the wrong way!"

"Awh…ahh," was her only response.

I told her about finding the room just steps ahead, and asked her if she could make it. A small nod gave me the okay to get her up. We would be there in just a few minutes. My mind was troubled as I wondered if the door to our refuge was still open.

We cautiously passed the lantern, which I would retrieve later.

"Just a few more steps now," were my encouraging words to my life-long buddy and partner in many a crime.

The other flashlight, tied to my shoe, caught the shimmer from the broken one I had strategically placed to mark the door. My eyes scanned the wall for an opening. Pre-occupied, I took another step closer. Oh no, my flashlight came loose from my shoe and I heard it drop. Making sure not to move, my eyes scanned in the direction of the light. There it was, two steps down and still working.

"Oh we are so lucky."

Mac sat on the step while I picked up the flashlight, our only light, and secured it tightly to my runner once more.

I picked up my broken marker flashlight, from in front of the door, only after opening it once more.

"Here we go Mac, you will be okay.

CHAPTER 9

In Our Refuge

How did we miss the downward tunnel the first time, I wondered. We were so focused on going up that we totally missed the other direction.

I put Mac on the floor. Then I moved the crate over the water pool by lifting the barrel, and of course, the door to the stairs closed too. It was the same entrance we used the other night. The door must close by itself. I thought we would have to be much more observant in the future.

Quickly I retrieved the sleeping bag, blanket and pillow from its tidy storage, and laid Mac down on one of the boxes. It made a nice bench to rest on.

Covering her, I took my light and shone it in her eyes. The pupils looked better, but I hoped all the strain wouldn't hurt her. She closed her eyes immediately after. I put pressure on her gash and she winced under my hand. After that, I applied some ointment. She would be fine now, but would need to regain her strength. I sat not knowing what I should do next. If I had the lantern I could have looked at some of the drawings we found.

As quickly as the thought came, I wanted to act on it. I couldn't leave Mac without light and only had one working flashlight. I decided to work on the broken one. After shaking and knocking it in my hand, it flickered.

Okay, it is just a loose contact somewhere.

After all the moving parts were tightened, suddenly it stayed on. It was as good as new except for a round chrome decorative piece that was missing. Relieved, I left it beside Mac, and left it on. I was relieved that the pool was covered as Mac was so disoriented and I needed to keep her safe. Now, would the door open by just tipping the barrel, but without leaving the pool of water exposed?

I pushed hard but nothing worked. Maybe I needed another approach. I was leaning on the wall behind the barrel and in my frustration, kicked it hard. The mysterious barrel tipped, teetered and settled back in the upright position.

Yes, it tipped if pushed the other way!

Anticipation was mounting as I wondered if that would open the door only. With the barrel on the floor, the door was wide open once more! I would retrieve the lantern and be right back. It would only take a minute.

CHAPTER 10

Locked Out

I was out the door and down the stairs, clutching my flashlight. Determination energized every step. Halted in my tracks by a large growl, I realized all was not well. That was the cat. It wouldn't come all this way, would it? I hurried as I could see the soft glow of the lantern below.

There it was again. "GRRRRAR!"

"Hurry, hurry," played over and over in my mind. I reached for the lantern and after picking it up I made a beeline up the stairs. It wouldn't be long and I would be safe even if the cat was tracking me all this way.

Where was the door? It was closed and had disappeared! I should have marked the step below the door. What a fool I was. I checked the wall carefully as I moved, holding my lantern high. My flashlight was now safe in my pouch.

There was a faint clang of metal, as with my next step, my foot hit something on the rock stair. Looking down to see what it was, my eyes caught the glimmer of a round chrome circle. It was the missing piece of the flashlight. I picked it up and put it in my pocket. This had to be where the door was. This is where I found my flashlight when it fell.

Franticly scanning the wall and feeling for something to move I pushed with all my might. Suddenly my body went flying into the room as the door opened.

There stood Mac ready to kill me.

She had remembered how to open the door! Of course, only after her panic attack, when she realized she was alone.

"Did you open the door?" I shouted.

"Yes I did!"

"Good job, and just in time. Close it quickly!"

Of course, it closed automatically and quickly.

"I heard the cat again and it sounded close!" I shouted.

"It is!" She questioned, "All this distance?"

We were safe now and could wait here for a while. We had all weekend to be at our friends' houses, or so our parents thought.

I knew Mac was feeling better when she asked, "Can we eat something? I am starved."

"You can't keep a good person down," I laughed.

My eyes scanned the shelves for a container to retrieve some water. I moved the huge crate to fill it, satisfied that the amount was sufficient for both of us for a while.

"Hey, did you test the water?"

"I sure did, it was gone and the cat was still alive when we got back with Dad," was my reply

"You gave it to your cat?"

"She's alive, isn't she?"

As my taste buds were trying to discern if the water tasted good, I started to gag, cough and choke.

When I caught a glance of the horror on Mac's face, I stopped, apologized and said, "It's good."

She had some too, and seemed to enjoy every drop.

"How about some pork and beans? I will even heat them up for you."

"No, how about some macaroni and cheese?"

"Okay," was my reply as I brought out the old Coleman stove. The naphtha gas canister needed to be pumped and then it could be lit with a match. I was glad Dad taught me how to use the Coleman properly.

We put some water in a small pot and waited for it to boil. The macaroni wouldn't take too long to cook, and was going to taste so good. We could hardly wait. The cheese was a little lumpy and dry, as we had no butter. Mac was clever enough to use a little water instead of milk when she saw how chunky it was. It became quite palatable and we enjoyed it to the last spoonful.

Mac cleaned up after boiling some more water for washing dishes, and found the six-inch hole in the corner to pour the dirty water in. It worked well and ran off quickly.

I kept myself occupied by looking at some of the old plans. Deciding to mark the ones already looked at, I took paper and pencil from the box.

CHAPTER 11

The Plans

Mac asked," How long have we been down here?"

I made a quick calculation in my head.

"About 19 hours. It's almost noon, 12:09 to be exact."

"No wonder I could have eaten an elephant."

"I am glad you didn't say a wild cat," I replied.

The first plan was of property lines. It looked like the park on the other side of the ravine. It was labeled, *Government Project of Queenston*. Our property was just above the escarpment near the project. There were four phases marked on the government project, two sections along the road, and two, along the gorge and river.

After marking it with a check mark I went on to the next one. This one made no sense at all. It had lines drawn every which way and had no rhyme or reason. That was a favorite saying of both Pa and Dad. They were always looking for things to make sense.

Mac had walked over and was looking over my shoulders.

"Hey that is the drawing of that huge black cave we were in. See the crevice on top where the moon shone in?"

"Yeah, I can see it now, that's cool. You have to stare at it awhile and it appears."

The sketch consisted of short pencil strokes and the cave was difficult to make out until you focused on it. Then it was clear and you couldn't help but see it.

"Well maybe you ... have to stare at it," she snickered, "but I don't."

As we had already devoured the packaged macaroni, I had thought that we should replace everything that we had used. We were thankful for the choice of food on the shelves and made a list of the items to be replaced.

Everything was put back in its place and it all looked tidy again. Boy, our Moms would be shocked at us. We even impressed ourselves. No one would have known we were here.

Opening the door to exit, our determination grew to find the opener from the tunnel side. We stepped into the tunnel with our lantern. We could barely see the very faint glow from the light above because of the turns in the tunnel. Where is that moveable part of this wall? We needed to mark it for next time. We couldn't find it anywhere when Mac said maybe it was on the door itself, and it was now pushed to the side, out of site.

We decided that Mac should go back in and I would keep the lantern with me. She should open the door in 10 minutes if I couldn't. I gave her my watch and, of course, my flashlight. She closed the door from the inside. I raised my lantern and searched and searched. Going over my steps once more I realized I was bending down when I pushed the wall.

Okay let's try that again. I encouraged myself.

Scanning and pushing the bottom of the wall I pushed along its width.

I felt a rock jut out just about an inch. I pushed on it. It moved and the door was open.

Congrats were in order and Mac made a big deal about it. We were pleased to accomplish what we set out to do. We had to think of something that would mark the place. We left the lantern in our hideaway and closed the door.

"Do you have your flashlight," I asked.

"Oh, I forgot it."

I figured it was safe until the next visit. Oh well, we would leave one thing out of place.

As soon as we closed the door we counted our steps, going up towards the light in the tunnel. There were 150 steps to get us under the dim light on the wall, an easy number to remember but a tedious job to count them.

Next trip I would bring something to mark the door. We climbed past the light until we got to the gazebo exit, and after I pulled the switch it got black behind us.

With the light out it would be difficult to see the opening to the tunnel if you didn't know it was there. The tunnel entrance was on the side where the gazebo foundation was built into the hill. It was underground and little light reflected through the cracks in the old boards. It just looked dark. The foundation of the gazebo was totally exposed on the ravine side. This was convenient as you could walk along it, and then up to the carriage house and not be seen.

It was late afternoon by now and we needed to get back. Since her head had a bandage Mac needed to have a story to account for it. We hated to invent stories for our parents, but I didn't know how else to keep things secret until we could find out more. It would be so nice to be able to tell them the truth. Mac and I were not used to lying to our parents and the consequence would be harsh.

"How about you hit your head on a rock doing a cartwheel?"

That sounded lame. She wasn't worried and would come up with something. She thought we could take her bandage off and she would adjust her long hair so you couldn't see her injury. Mac promised she would go to the clinic before the day was done to get herself checked out. We would both be back in time for supper and that was all we needed to know for now. We didn't know when we would get back so we would have to be in touch by texting.

"Make sure your phone is charged, okay."

I replied with, "Will do."

I would walk Mac along the gorge until off our property. There was a well-trodden path that was carved by years of biking and continuous walking back and forth.

We enjoyed the sound of the running water on those hot nights as we spent time in the little family cemetery along our path. My Great-Granddad carefully designed it after the small gardener's house was torn down, and Pa redesigned it, so he said.

It looked quite ordinary to me, for an old cemetery. Pa's Dad was known as Opa Wittfoot. I guess his name kept all the Opas straight. I never knew him or my Great-Oma Wittfoot, but heard many stories of their lives.

I got to know my Omz, Dad's mom. She was also buried here in our little cemetery. It was only a few years since she passed but I remembered her energy in playing with us as well as the fragrance in the house from her German cooking.

I involved Mac in our German traditions at Christmas including the pickle on the Christmas tree, marzipan, and the celebration on Christmas Eve after attending our church service. Mac and Mark took part in many of our family traditions, including eating the coveted Halva.

Mark also grew up with some of the same traditions, while Mac had many of her own Dutch ones.

With all the reminiscing, we got to Mac's in no time.

I went as far as I could without being seen and Mac would make it from there.

CHAPTER 12

Dad Lets Me In

I quietly walked into the back door of the coach house.

Mom and Dad were talking intensely and I heard Dad say, "I need to protect them. They can't know."

Mom gave a loud sigh and agreed although she did not know all the secrets.

"Look at what happened to Dad. I am sure they are behind his disappearance.

It will all be over when the house is torn down. There will be no guessing."

"What was that supposed to mean and when was that happening? Dad sure knew more than he was saying. He needed to know what I knew, or did he already know that?

I opened the door again and slammed it as though I had just stepped in.

"Hi Mom, hi Dad, what's for supper?"

"Josh you look like you slept in those clothes. What were you and Mark doing? Never mind, just get changed before dinner and put your stuff in the laundry basket, okay?"

"Will do," was my reply as I turned to go.

Dad noticed my pouch and commented as how much I wore it, and that Pa would have enjoyed knowing that. His brow furrowed and his face became sad as he spoke and realized what he had said.

I told him I missed Pa too, and we could talk about him more, as I too had so many meaningful memories.

He sighed, with a couple of nods, and Mom smiled in agreement.

In my room, I changed, and was careful to put my supply list on my dresser in a little box Pa gave me years ago. He always said it was special and could tell me many new things.

"Okay, Pa, I want to know now," I mumbled to myself. I dumped it and looked carefully at it like it would talk to me. It was covered with soft hand-painted leather graphics.

I turned it over and thought that they meant nothing to me.

What could I learn? I shook it and to my surprise I felt a small movement inside. Just then Mom came into the room and said supper was ready. She saw the emptied box and wondered what I was doing.

"I am just cleaning this thing out," I told her.

It certainly needed it.

"Come and eat, Josh you can finish that later."

How was I going to eat now? Forcing myself to sit at the table, Dad reminded me of what I said about Pa. He wanted to tell me something and it would be our secret. He kept the conversation light during dinner, as he knew what my reaction would be to his news. We went outside after supper as we used to do and talked.

Sighing again, Dad started, "Pa was working on something very important when he disappeared. He had a lot of secrets, some he told me of and others not. He said the house would show me how to find him, in case something happened to him. It has been vacant for over a year since Pa disappeared, and I have been through every inch of the house, and still found nothing. I am an investigator and have been able to come up with nothing! I feel defeated Josh. All I can do is have the house torn down, and maybe then I can find some answers."

Mom came out to join us with a cup of tea, as she often enjoyed the evening air, just as I was exploding.

"No Dad, don't, I can help you, please don't."

"I know you think you can, but you are too young and I have nowhere to turn."

"Dad, come with me right now and I will prove it to you."

"Josh I know you think you can but ..."

"Dad I will show you how the house can tell you."

I forgot all about the box in my room and was targeting my thoughts at Dad and what I could show him.

"I think you should at least give him a chance," Mom softly pleaded like only a Mom can.

"Yeah Dad, I will prove it to you," I said. "Come with me. I'll get my flashlight," and I jumped up and ran in for my pouch.

"It will only take a minute and we will be back, can we clean up from supper then?"

"Certainly, I can keep dessert for later. He sure is excited about helping you. Please be careful. I will put some dinner aside for Bee. She will be home in a while."

—~—

Dad wasn't expecting much but was willing to let me lead.

"Do you want to go through the house Dad or the gazebo?" I asked.

"What?"

"We should go through the house so it can show you it's secrets, okay?"

"Sounds good, Son."

With our flashlights in hand, we entered the ravine side French door from the porch. I motioned for Dad to come over to the closet, as he protested. He had checked the closet maybe a hundred times. I stood him against the wall and pushed him into it, and the wall opened. As we walked in Dad was shocked.

"How did you find this?"

Motioning again for him to follow me, I noticed this time he was glad to oblige. My light was scanning the wall for that nail.

"Okay Dad stand close in front of me." I pulled on the nail to bring out the board. The floor fell from beneath us and we were off.

"Hold onto your flashlight Dad!" I shouted. Twisting and turning, we came to an abrupt halt with me on top of Dad. I knew better than to stand in front of him.

When Dad realized what had happened he was in a kind of a

trance. Coming to his senses again, he wanted to know all about this place, and, of course, how I found it. I told him I used to hide in the secret hall with Mac, but only found the slide a couple of days ago.

I switched on the lantern and he had a good look around.

"Dad, watch this," I said as I went over to the barrel and turned it so that the crate exposed the water pool by moving aside. I showed him how to work the door. He was astonished to learn about the door, which was 150 steps from the light, leading to the opening above. I also showed him how to open it from the tunnel side.

He couldn't believe I had discovered all of this by myself. I was afraid to tell him that Mac also knew, because of the danger Dad talked about. I told him about the wild cat and how I had barricaded myself in a small cave and closed it up with a huge rock from inside.

I also remembered to tell him the door shut automatically if left alone.

I showed him the Coleman stove, the supplies, the sleeping bag, pillow and blanket, the gunpowder, and lastly, the drawings. Dad was excited, and said I had done an awesome job figuring this out.

"Who do you think is using this place Dad?"

He answered, "Let's try to find out."

I showed him the old typewriter and Dad's face went pale.

"It's only an old typewriter Dad, not to worry."

After sitting he said, "That was Pa's old typewriter."

I wondered how it got down here.

Dad was now on a mission, and asked, "What did Pa have to do with this place down here? This was just the kind of tidy storage room that your Pa would have had.

"There is one thing missing in his food supply. It can't have been your pa's."

He picked up things and put them back, studying the contents of the shelves.

"What would that be, Dad?"

"Your Pa once told me that if he had a supply room he would have a macaroni dinner, known as 'KD' or 'Mac 'n' Cheese' in it."

With eyes wide and popping out of my head I shouted, "It does

Dad, I mean, it did until we ate it!"

"You ate it with who?"

The cat was out of the bag and I had to fess up, and told him that Mac was down here with me two times and we enjoyed the Mac 'n' Cheese. With a smirk that quickly turned serious he wondered if it was a good idea for Mac to know about this place. I confessed that Mac knew about the hiding spot in the house for many years, and had never told anyone.

He said that he felt reassured once more and we returned to our thoughts about Pa. How could he live down here for so long without us knowing?

"Let's see, if this was Pa's work why did he need it?

Who was he hiding from and where is he now?"

"Let's have a look at those drawings, Son. Are they numbered somehow?"

"I don't know, I never thought of that, Dad."

We looked at some that were new to me. They didn't seem to have numbers or any kind of sequence, but had letters on the sides. The one we were looking at had *fünf* on it.

"What could that mean?" Dad asked.

Something looked familiar about the letter.

"Hey Dad, isn't that German. Pa had some letters typed in German, didn't he?"

"I didn't look at the letters as a word but yes; it is the number five in German. Pa taught me to read the numbers from one to ten in his native tongue.

Good work, and where are the letters on the box?"

I showed him, "Over here, on the other side."

"It says from Germany to Canada," Dad mumbled, "and what is this very small writing in the corner?"

We could hardly make it out but we read "Witt" with some other letters.

We will need a magnifying glass to read it. Telling Dad we make lists of our supply needs, I went for the paper and pencil and wrote down magnifying glass.

"Oh Dad, I forgot my list on my dresser beside my box from Pa. Oh yeah! I forgot to tell you! When I dumped it to search for something, I heard and felt movement in it. I didn't have time to check it out because Mom came in and wanted me for supper."

Dad assured me that we would be certain to turn that box inside out if we had to.

"Pa told me he would make sure you had the key, Josh. I didn't want to ask you because I thought maybe he didn't have a chance to give you the clues before he disappeared. I have checked your pouch a thousand times and found nothing. I didn't realize Pa gave you that box too."

"I know Dad, he told me not to tell anyone where I got it."

"Really ... I don't believe it; you know I have been all over the world following every lead of communication Pa ever made. All the times the clues where right here under my nose."

That is why we could not demolish the old mansion. It had the clues to many secrets and maybe even to the disappearance of Pa.

As Dad looked at his watch, his face showed worry as those brows furrowed once more.

"Your mother is going to be worried. We have been down here for hours."

"I know the time seems to get away from me whenever I am down here," I replied.

We made a pact to start out first thing in the morning, tomorrow after breakfast, bringing the supplies we needed and investigate. For now, we would go back and try to contain our excitement.

"Dad does Mom ... I mean can we talk in front of Mom?"

"Yes you can but no one else, do you understand, no one else. It could be dangerous. Your Pa told me to be very careful."

"Okay, got it."

We were careful to put everything back as we found it and I led Dad up the stairs to the gazebo, using our flashlights. He was impressed with my every move and I enjoyed being the leader as he followed me upward. I pointed out the one hundred and fifty stairs to the light. We agreed that the secret door should be marked next time in an inconspicuous way. He agreed and we finally arrived under the gazebo.

I showed him the inaccessible cliff door and our new escape. He didn't fit through the removed boards as well as Mac and I did, but he was barely able to manage thanks to his new smaller physique. Looking to see if all was clear we made our way around the gazebo stairs towards the house.

There were lights flashing and sirens. *What now?*

"Dad we will have to say that we were jogging or something."

"Well we are not all sweaty so let's say we were walking the ridge path, just if anyone asks, okay?"

"Alright, but..."

" I wouldn't worry about it Josh, no one will ask."

All the action was at the end of our lane where the driveway met the old river road.

CHAPTER 13

The Accident—Not!

I got a sick feeling in the pit of my stomach as we spoke in unison, "Let's go see what happened!"

The lights were flashing on an ambulance, fire truck and three police cars. What was happening? As we neared I saw Mom crying in a policeman's arms. They had the road blocked and were trying to get someone out of the overturned car.

Dad started to run to Mom. She threw herself into his arms.

"It's Bee—she's in there."

"Did you talk to her?"

"No they won't let me near the car," she sobbed.

"Josh, take care of your mom."

I took my place as Mom's comforter as I always did when Dad was away.

Dad argued with the police until he was allowed to move in closer.

He called, "Bee, Bee. Can you say something? Let me know if you are okay."

He could hear a weak voice.

"Thank you, God," Dad cried out.

She was hanging in the air. Her seat belt was keeping her head off of the ground.

"Bee can you feel your feet…your arms…your head?"

"Yes I think so."

"Good, we will have you out of there in no time." He shouted as the strong odor caught his attention. "I smell gas!"

Dad jumped into action, as he crawled through the window on the passenger side, followed by shouts from the police, warning him not to go inside. There are times you have to do what you have to do, no matter what anyone else says. This was one those times.

He was careful to support her weight, and put his knees under Bee so she wouldn't fall on her head. He slid his body under Bee's for support.

"Are you still okay?" As he struggled with it, her seat belt finally loosened.

"I'm okay now, Dad."

Dad gently planted one of those natural Dad kisses on her forehead and said, "Let's get out of here."

He slid his body forward just a little to support hers, as the paramedic on the outside put a stretcher board inside the window. Dad slid her onto it as it was pushed in further. She was carefully placed on the stretcher.

"Okay she is ready."

They pulled the stretcher out carefully with Dad lifting it on the inside. When she was free Mom went running to be with her. Dad crawled out quickly, as the firemen kept the car from exploding.

Mom rode in the ambulance with Bee and I drove to the hospital with Dad after he exchanged a few words with the officer in charge.

What could have happened went through our minds, repeatedly. Bee was a conscientious driver and always erred on the side of caution. Bee would tell us everything as soon as she got a chance. They were going to examine her at the hospital. I knew Bee would be okay; she had to be.

The ambulance took Bee to the Niagara Falls hospital, which was the closer one. Dad called a doctor friend of his to meet the ambulance, as he wanted to take no chances.

Bee was comfortable and was being checked by Dr. John Schultz who worked closely with Dr. Gerard in their clinic. Both were excellent doctors but John was a friend, and our family doctor.

He explained that everything looked good but he wanted to make sure there were no internal injuries and she would have to be admitted for the night.

"I knew her mother would want to stay with her, so I made arrangements for a cot."

"Thank you," came from Dad with a furrowed brow.

Can we see her now?" I asked.

"Of course you can, and we will let you know in the morning what the test results show.

When we walked in Mom was holding Bee, who was sobbing. I guess the shock was wearing off and the reality of the situation had set in.

Dad sat on the edge of the bed opposite to Mom and I just stood there and took it all in. This was serious; Bee could have been killed tonight.

The reality hit me like a ton of bricks, and I turned pale. I was a fair kid and when I got pale I got white. Mom looked up at me and told me to sit and put my head down on my lap. Feeling totally out of it as if in another world, I was glad to oblige. It took a while before I entered the real world. Feeling better, I zeroed in on the conversation again.

Bee said she was coming home after dropping Carly off at her house. Near to the point of turning onto our driveway she saw headlights suddenly glaring in front of her. A vehicle was coming her way, on her side of the road, and speeding. She did not know what to do except turn sharply to the side, away from it. She thought it could have been a truck, but it all happened so fast. The vehicle hit her at the back, driver's side.

She went flying as the car overturned.

She got teary eyed and said," I thought I was going to die."

With pleading moist eyes she said, "The other vehicle must have got away. I promise that's what happened. The dark monster was coming straight for me, the driver, but I turned sharply away from it. It is all a fog, and I don't know anything else until I heard you call my name, Dad."

She must have blacked out. We told her we loved her, believed her and were so glad she was not hurt more than she was. We assured her she was in fact safe now, and that she had nothing to worry about.

The police would find the truck, if it was a truck that hit her. We also surmised the driver was probably drunk, although it was of no consolation to any of us.

We said our good nights just as they were bringing in a cot for Mom to sleep on, but I knew full well that was not going to happen.

Dad slipped out for a couple of minutes and when he came back he seemed ready to let the girls get some rest. He had his suspicions that this accident was as deliberate as Omz's was and was mentally trying to put it all together.

CHAPTER 14

Back in the Carriage House

As we drove through the now sleeping city, it felt solemn and lonely. Its past excitement had vanished and it was a quiet ride home. There were so many things to talk about and yet neither one of us could bring ourselves to utter a word about them. It seemed like our words were imprisoned, never to escape. When we came from our secret room we had purpose and knew exactly what the next step was going to be. Now we seemed lost and it was difficult to give word to the thoughts scrambling in our heads.

As we neared the driveway we could see the police still trying to determine clues as to the colour or make of the offending vehicle. The tow truck was waiting to pull Bee's car away as soon as they were finished.

With a nod of his head, Dad drove by them as he turned into our laneway, past the stone pillars that guarded the entrance.

"It's a good thing she didn't hit those pillars," I mumbled.

"It sure is," Dad replied as he parked the car inside the garage of our home.

The lights were still on and you could tell by the kitchen that it was abandoned in a hurry.

"Do you think someone was waiting for Bee?" I asked.

"To be honest with you, the thought had crossed my mind too. Let's not let our imaginations run wild and stick to the facts when they come in." Dad replied.

With great reluctance, we decided to eat something, and put the leftovers in the fridge. Mom had made Bee's favorite tonight, Fettuccine Alfredo. As we cleaned the kitchen and readied it for the next day our thoughts came back to the hours before.

"Dad, let's go and see what the box has to tell us."

Almost running to my room and Dad following close behind, we stopped cold in or tracks. My parents' room was totally torn apart. Every drawer was dumped and dressers where overturned.

The mattress was on its side and clothes were everywhere.

Who did this? A cold chill ran down my spine. I felt like someone was still in the house.

"Do you think someone is still here? "

Dad shook his head, no, and started to check the other rooms. They seemed to be untouched. This was too much of a coincidence, and I hoped that my box was still there. I ran to my room and Dad almost tackled me. He motioned with his finger over his mouth, to make no sound. He took some paper and wrote on it. Someone might be listening. He told me to get what I needed and pointed to the box and list and said we would go where we can talk.

We talked normally so as not to tip someone off and said we should try to get some sleep and start early to clean up the mess. No sense calling the police as it was probably some juveniles in the area trying to find some fast money.

I grabbed the fluorescent tape, my pouch, the box and whatever else I could think of, and turned off my light.

Dad said good night Son, and I responded, "Good night Dad."

He said he would go and turn the lights off, and I said, "Okay."

He strategically turned all the lights off and we snuck out of the back door without making a sound. This time Dad locked the door, and made our way along the ravine, until we got to the gazebo, once again.

"I think we should look in Pa's study Dad. Pa said there were two exits and I have never found the other. It is in the middle of the house and no one will see the lights of the lamps."

Dad thought it was a great idea and we made our way up the incline, from the gazebo path to the back porch of the house. This part of the porch facing the water had its own charm. It had the original grand wicker rocking chairs still where they used to be in years gone by. You could tell by their worn appearance they had been the center of many, many family conversations and evenings with guests. Two sets of French doors to the great room allowed lots of moonlight to guide our steps.

CHAPTER 15

The Study

We made our way into the back room, where the bookcases, acting as secret doors, provided access to the study.

One difference was that everyone in the family knew about the study and how to get in. This was not a secret to our family; nevertheless it was intriguing to everyone else who entered the study through the bookcase.

"Pa loved this secret stuff didn't he Dad?"

"Seems that way, but I know for a fact he did it for his safety and ours."

I still didn't know what the danger was and why, so I asked. Dad again said he would tell me when we were in a very safe place.

We closed the bookcase behind us, and once more felt that cocooned feeling. Dad said he hadn't been in there, since he searched for clues months ago, before leaving to investigate, but everything was just as he remembered.

The whole mansion was just as Omz and Pa had left it.

"Pa never did get rid of a single thing."

I nodded and put my box on the leather inlay of the refined looking antique desk. Beside it carefully placed was my duct tape and pouch. I sat in Pa's aged office chair. It looked at home in the old study just as you would imagine. Large antique brass nail studs adorned its high back and interesting shape, with arms designed to guard its inhabitant.

I flipped the box upside down and right side up and listened for some movement. I heard nothing. Then I shook it again and there it was.

"Listen Dad!" I whispered.

He was attentive as I shook the seemingly empty box. There *was* something in there, and we had to figure out how to retrieve it without tearing the box to shreds. Dad said, "Let me have a good look at that, I have never seen it up close before." He studied the pictures for the first time.

Surprised, he pointed out the tiny picture of the neat storage room.

I was blown away as I didn't realize it was on there. The picture was so small, and was just one of many that made a collage covering for the box.

"That is so cool," I whispered, and checked to see what else I would recognize.

There was a picture of the study. It had the two chairs in each corner, the antique leather top desk and chair, and the old hutch on the far wall.

Even the outdated dark wood paneling was drawn in miniature detail. Pa's old clock was on the shelf with his Dad's aged Bible, both beside an old typewriter. It looked just like the one I found in the storage room. I wondered where the Bible and the clock were as I concentrated on the empty shelf in the study: no clock or Bible.

I would catch Pa many evenings reading it in his study. He said it was too bad I didn't know German. He would have loved me to have that old Bible to enjoy as he did. He also emphasized, it was the best guide for his life, and mine.

Back to checking out my box, I found the tiniest picture of the cougar. It was on the bottom of the box.

Dad looked and said, "Have you seen this...large...cavern yet?"

It was the picture beside the cougar. "Yes, that one is just before you get outside, where we saw the cougar. Wow, look at this nice room. Boy it can't be here. It must be a decoy picture."

There were sketches of tunnels, stairs and even a lake in a huge cavern.

We decided to open the box. It had to have a false bottom. Carefully, Dad tried to remove the bottom from the inside but it didn't come up.

Dad said he knew where Pa's office tools were, where he kept a nice sharp knife. Hopefully it was still there. He used the flashlight to look into the drawer, as the lamp was on the desk. He started pushing stuff around.

Something made a clang as it fell out at the back of the drawer. I guess it needed some repair; after all, this hutch was quite old.

First, he stuck his hand into the drawer to see where he heard the clang. The back of the drawer was missing and he found a hollow space. That was odd. Then, he pulled the drawer out and shone the flashlight into it.

"Take a look Josh!"

I peered in, and it looked like there was a space back there.

"How do we…?" I asked, and Dad stopped me.

"Shhh."

He put his hand inside and felt for something metallic at the end of the drawer cavity. He pulled it and the supply cabinet moved away from the wall. He quickly had to take a step back.

He signaled me to gather my stuff and turn the light off. Of course, I hurried, so excited that we found the other exit.

Dad had me go ahead with the light while he grabbed the drawer and put it back. He had to hurry to slip in before it closed behind us.

CHAPTER 16

The Study Escape

We both had our flashlights in our hands and shone them around us. We were in a space the size of a walk-in closet.

We should have checked how to get out of here before we closed the door. We looked for something, anything!

"Dad, here on the floor is a key hole!"

"Maybe the key is in the box?" Dad suggested.

"I have my jackknife and we can cut the bottom, or the bottom from the inside."

I dug for my knife and gave it to Dad. He put the box on the floor and cut into the edges not too deeply, but all the way around. Nothing moved, or lifted. While I was holding the flashlight for him I had time to stare down into the box and noticed a picture of a key on the inside.

We decided to cut the picture out and see if the key was under it. The knife cut around three sides of the picture and it seemed to cut easily. Dad carefully pried it open. There, in a narrow, two-inch long space, with very little room for movement, was a key. I hoped it would work for us.

We grabbed all of our stuff and put it in our pockets, except for our flashlights. We knew the floor could give way or open in some other fashion. No one knew to what, or where.

The key went in and nothing happened. Dad turned it and still nothing happened. When he tried to get it out of the keyhole the board seemed to lift. He told me to stand behind him and he tried again. This time the section of floor lifted. He grabbed the key and lifted it up as high as it would go. A set of stairs that led down appeared.

When we got to the bottom the trap door closed and the sidewall opened. We went in hoping to get to our storage room.

As the wall closed, Dad said, "A lot more stairs."

"Did you see some kind of hinge on those doors?" he added.

"I wasn't looking for that," was my reply.

The stairs were now cut into the stone and tunneled in a twisting fashion all the while going down.

"I think this is further than the storage room, or maybe it is twisting more Dad."

"I just hope we get back by the morning," Dad replied.

When we finally reached the bottom, in front of us stood an oversized wooden door. We pushed it, banged it, knocked on it, but nothing worked. I had an idea. *The wall upstairs works like this.* I stood in front of it and leaned slightly into it with pressure from my body, and guess what—it didn't work.

We studied it again with our flashlights and there, we found another keyhole. Dad inserted the same key we used upstairs and turned it. The old plank door opened with a loud creak.

"Look at this!" Dad said as the door was pushed all the way open.

It was awesome! You just would not believe this; no one would unless they saw it with their own eyes.

CHAPTER 17

Unbelievable

Our flashlights caused an air raid effect, searching the room for something unseen.

It was a large room-like, cavern, about thirty feet high and maybe the size of a couple of very, very, large bedrooms.

"Did you ever see anything like this?"

"Can't say that I have," replied Dad, ". . . except on your box."

We were so taken up with our find that Dad forgot to take the key out until I yelled, "Don't close the door. Get the key."

He was grateful and pulled it out. We thought we would keep the door ajar and put a chair in between to jam it. Upon examining the door from the inside, we realized the same key worked to lock or unlock it from the inside as well.

This place was like one you would read about in a novel. Our flashlights slowly brought everything to light. At first glance my eyes caught sight of animal furs hanging on the walls. There were many. The glass from three old lamps, on an ancient hutch, reflected the light from my flashlight. There were three huge old fur rugs on the stone floor, making the coziest-looking room I had ever seen. An old table that appeared to have layers of chipped paint giving way to small splashes of colour stood to our left.

Four chairs, once nicely painted, accompanied it.

Against the wall just past the table and chairs stood an old hutch containing odds and ends of dishes, as well as the lanterns. The two large bear furs behind the hutch made a cozy backdrop for it. We couldn't believe our eyes, and decided to put the lamps on, so we could get a better look. We noticed there was another Coleman stove all set up and ready to be used.

Who lived down here?

We took a few minutes to adjust to our new surroundings. The old, over-sized crate imitating a coffee table was dusty and bare. The loungers were a set, but only in style, not in colour. They were torn in spots and one was, or used to be, a deep green while the other looked a fleshy rose.

I noticed the solid wood crate also had the same script that the ones in the storage room had. It definitely was out of proportion as a coffee table and my eyes were drawn to it over and over again. My limitations in the field of design hindered my accurate criticism, but this just looked wrong.

The place was a cave, but kind of like a hideout. My mind went back to my buddy, Mark. He and I could have so much fun in here.

"Dad could I use this for a club house some day?"

"We must find out what it is used for and who uses it, Son, but maybe some day."

My mind just went wild at the thoughts of Mark and I living down here. That would be so cool. We would have to let Mac visit sometimes, of course.

She could always be one of the gang when she wanted to be, although lately she seemed to be turning into a girl at times. Her moods would change out of the blue, and Mark and I were totally in the dark as to what to do with them. When I heard Dad's voice, it snapped me back to reality.

Dad said that he thought we should check the perimeter, and see if it led anywhere else. Every room had two exits and I was more convinced about that than ever. Pa said it, and so far it had been true; some rooms had even more than two.

We each took a lantern and shone the light on the walls as we took a close look. Dad went one way and I the other.

There were a few more animal furs hanging on the walls. I felt them as I walked past them. One was so soft, and the fur was thick and white. It was definitely a polar bear fur although the head was missing. You could see the long razor-like claws, which looked as though they were clinging to the rock wall. The next one had short hair and it jerked my fingers as they slid over it against the grain. It definitely was a zebra fur. Not by the feel but the black and white striped design giving it away. Anyone would be able to recognize that one.

I was interrupted by Dad's anxious sound.

"This is your pa's clock. What is it doing down here?"

I went and had a good look at it, remembering it was Pa's favorite clock. It sounded a full and traditional chime when wound up. I checked and the chime button was off.

"Do you think Pa was down here?'

"I just don't know."

"Then that must have been his typewriter in the storage room."

CHAPTER 18

The Talk

Dad plunked himself down on the old recliner with discouragement all over his face. The thought of Pa being down here at one time, and not knowing where he was now, was overwhelming.

"Dad can you tell me about how my Great-Opa and Oma came to this country?" I assumed they brought the crates over to Canada.

I sat beside him and he started talking. He would tell me what he knew, but said there was a lot that he was denied access to.

"Your Great-Opa and Oma Wittfoot came from Germany right after the war. Great-Opa had been in charge of a wagon train of German people escaping the Russians during the war. Since they were Germans living in Russia, the Russians would have captured them and sent them to Siberia. They were afraid that the Germans would side with Hitler and rebel to further the cause of this tyrant.

"They fled through many countries and ended up in Germany right after the war. All the while your Great-Opa nurtured and directed the wagon train to safety. They worked for their food rations and did odd jobs wherever they could. Babies were born along the way, while others died giving in to the hardships they endured."

Other countries did not like the Germans either, understandably so, I surmised, because of what Hitler did.

"Your Opa Wittfoot also did not like Hitler for what he had done to his people and even his relatives. Many were taken to prison, for standing their ground, where they died, and some were never heard from again. The country was in utter devastation. Opa decided to move to Canada, taking only his immediate family—his wife, your Oma and your Pa, their son. They also took five large carefully packed crates. That was a lot of cargo for immigrants in those days as most came over with just one or two crates. Opa's family belongings had been collected by Great-Opa and Oma as his family were imprisoned. They did not want to leave all these belongings behind as they were entrusted in their care."

"Well I guess we have found all the crates now," I interjected. I wondered what was in them. Three crates were left sealed even until I was a child.

They were literally keeping them for someone until their return. After one of Pa's trips to Europe, he and Omz decided to open them. It was like Christmas for me! I was so intrigued. All my life, I saw the boxes stacked on top of one another and stored in one of our spare bedrooms. I never stopped wondering what was in them. Their contents were finally being revealed.

One box was filled with some papers, the old Bible, and bedding. It contained hand- embroidered tablecloths and hand-made doilies. I recall helping them unpack the other one. It contained the old typewriter, clock and the three old lanterns. There were other items too. Some kitchen accessories, pots and pans, ladles and serving spoons.

The dishes in Omz's and Pa's house were the original ones brought from Europe. Omz loved using these items, as it was a nice reminder of her family. The contents were precious as they traveled so far and these belongings gave a lot of security as they could be sold for food during the war. I remembered making such a mess with all the protecting straw from the crates and spreading it throughout the house.

They would only part with these items if it became necessary.

When Opa arrived in Canada he was hired by the government to investigate a plot to destroy the power plant in Queenston, on the Niagara River.

He did this undercover and lived as a gardener and hired hand. His native tongue was German and he was a self-taught English-speaking immigrant, which was a great asset. He was in the police force back in the old country as well. The government was afraid that even though the war was over, there would be retaliation. The spying had revealed a plan, even a year before the war started.

Opa learned about the group behind the threat, and how it sent its information back and forth. The government received names and times of exchanges. He obtained information that a lot of money had been smuggled into the country to finance this endeavor, before the war ended. It also financed a spy ring here in Canada and the United States.

He didn't get as far as finding the money. The enemy discovered the research. The plot was immediately disbanded without warning and the spies were suddenly called back to Germany. They shut down their operation.

Before he could finish his investigation he was taken off the case and was even accused of being a spy himself. It devastated his view of this country that promised freedom and justice to all. The government bought that property next door, before we had this one. They turned it upside down and scoured the rock walls for clues to the money. The money was supposed to be there, but no one found it. At least it was never published that it was found. All the searching for money took place in secret, and no one knew about it.

It was common knowledge that smugglers would dock near the bridge to United States, right here in Queenston, below the escarpment. It is no longer there as it was torn down years ago.

Queenston was the place for shipments to be brought and stored away. Nothing was ever found. If you look at the lay of the land in Queenston you would find it the closet accessible landing area. Everyone travelling by boat to Niagara Falls would have to dock here and take horse and buggy the rest of the way.

This applied to St. David's and all the small communities around Niagara as well.

"The mansion stood as it does now except for some remodeling that your Opa and Oma did themselves. I will tell you about that later, Son. Your Great-Opa was also a talented wood craftsman and inventor. He had made good money in the government, until accused, but lived a modest lifestyle with your Great-Oma.

"She made everything from scratch as well as sewing her own clothes. She sold her baked goods in the nearest towns, Niagara Falls, Niagara on the Lake, Queenston, and St. David's. She did mending for others, and was kept very busy. The little gardener's house was a humble home and didn't take much time to maintain."

It was good for Dad to talk, as it took his mind off the work at hand.

"Your Pa grew up here from the time he was seven years old, when they came from Europe. The owners of this property let the family stay in the little garden house right where the cemetery is now, built for the gardener. Even though Great-Opa Wittfoot had become friends with the landlord, he still had to pay his rent and continually be "Mr. Fix It" for him.

Since the landlord was also German they could speak with each in their native tongue for many hours. The landlord was also grateful for the townspeople's trust, as they were highly skeptical of the German folk who were relative newcomers to their small community.

"Your Great-Opa and Oma of course being two of these newcomers, Josh."

"Your Great-Oma did the laundry, baking, and canning for her German landlady. The landlord hosted many great parties for the wealthy. The carriages would pull up to the wraparound porch and your Great-Granddad would help the elegantly clad ladies into the house. Your Great-Grandmother worked hard and long hours. As well as being on call when her landlord decided to have parties, she often entertained overnight guests. Your Great-Oma would prepare the meals as well as serve them, and clean up afterwards."

"When the owners of the mansion decided to suddenly go back to Germany they sold your Great-Opa the house for whatever savings they had been able to accumulate.

"Great-Opa said he knew that something was wrong, as the landlords were always nervous and suspicious. I guess, with all the bad feelings between the nations this nervousness would have been understandable."

It must have been so different for them to live in such a big home after living life in the confined borders of the gardener's cottage, having such a minimal footprint. There wasn't much to move into the mansion, as they had so few things. It had an unfinished cold look, so Pa said. He didn't enjoy living here then as a boy. They just kept on living their poor life style and left things exactly as they were. The bedrooms were left as well as the old cupboard, desk and chairs in the office. The house looked totally furnished, as the German landlord took nothing but boxes of personal items. The couple just added their humble furniture from the little cottage.

Opa Wittfoot was ridiculed and taunted for being a German spy. He was a recent arrival to Canada and neighbours didn't visit them. At times, they were shunned. The couple wondered why the former landlords had so many friends yet they did not although they were the same nationality. The conclusion drawn was that their money was the drawing card.

"Your Great-Opa spent a lot of time away from home by himself. No one knew or cared where he spent all those hours. We thought he was off puttering and enjoying himself. Pa said he now understood why Great-Opa was out of sight so much. He was doing research about the 'German secret mission.' He had to be discrete while gathering information."

Dad spoke reflectively, "When they passed away..."

"And only two days apart!" I interjected, "I heard bits and pieces of this story before," I also added.

"Yes that's right. Well Pa and Omz took over the mansion. They both lived in the mansion with Pa's parents since they got married two years prior, but of course they quickly adjusted to the style in which the parents had lived for years.

"Omz loved decorating and the home took on a new life. She knew how to make something out of nothing, and how to stretch a dollar. She made old furniture look stately, and gave the place a decorator's edge. She entertained her community and often invited her neighbours for coffee and afternoon teas.

"As time went on the spy rumours had become a thing of the past. They proved to be hard working and honourable citizens. Pa and Omz were upstanding members of their community and well respected, a far cry from the years of scrutiny his parents had endured.

"Your Pa insisted I go to Toronto University and I become a police investigator, with the proper documentation."

Dad sighed as if he couldn't catch his breath.

"Your Omz was so proud that I was following your Opa Wittfoot's profession. Pa never had a chance to get training as an investigator, but was in the police force. He, on the other hand, had the rare opportunity to learn so much from his dad.

"Your Omz's death was untimely. It happened one night when Pa was away working out of the country."

Dad continued, "Omz was driving home from a play in Niagara-on-the-Lake, at the historic Royal George Theatre. She was in charge of a fundraiser for the homeless that night and they had raised enough to provide many families with their special needs to recover from various financial calamities.

"Her car veered off the road and ended up in the gorge, killing her instantly. No one ever did find out why her car went over. There were no skid marks. It was as if she didn't know what hit her or where she was going. They couldn't figure it out. After a grueling and complicated recovery of the body, the car was found to have water on the inside and the passenger's seat was soaked.

"Investigators never did come to conclusions, even to this day. There were large puddles of water on the road and shoulders. It wasn't raining. There were no eyewitnesses and there was no evidence except for the wet passenger side of the car. It was a balmy night and Omz had her passenger window all the way down, enjoying the fresh night air.

"Your Pa made his way home immediately and I tried to hold things together until he arrived.

"Before Omz's accident Pa and Omz wanted us to live in the big house. We only lived here in Queenston just a couple of minutes away but the house was getting too much for my aging parents.

"Pa remodeled the coach house for himself and Omz. We watched him sell his old coaches to collectors, as he anticipated things would never be the same again. That took him a couple of years, and we were just about to move in when the accident happened.

"Of course, we did not want to upset Pa's life now and we moved into the coach house ourselves. I didn't want to bring it up until Pa was ready but he said when we moved to the big house he and I would have many discoveries to make. Oh, how I wish he would have shared more of his life and thoughts with me."

"I remember being here in the big house with Omz and how I could smell her baking. The soups she made, and the sauerkraut and sausage dinners were awesome! My favorite was the roll kuchen (a deep fried German pastry), sprinkled with all that icing sugar and those sweet juicy watermelons! I loved the red cabbage, and can still taste it. I wish we could make some, Dad. I remember sitting around that huge table in the dining hall, as Omz called it, enjoying our meal, accompanied by interesting discussion."

The thought entered my mind to get all her recipes and write a book. Her paska, or Easter bread, was a favorite of Bee's. Most of all I loved the laughing. Omz loved to see everyone laughing uncontrollably and would have her camera ready for those disgusting candid photos.

She was always covering for Pa, as we couldn't find him during the day.

"I think Omz knew where Pa was the whole time, don't you, Dad?"

My question snapped Dad back to reality and he replied, "Yes I do too."

Dad continued, "We spent a lot of time talking when he was home for the evenings. I wondered where he went during the day and what he did to keep so busy?"

Dad mused, with furrowed brow and added, "He confided in me, just weeks before he disappeared. He was close to discovering something big. I had no idea what."

I was just a kid but knew something didn't add up. Because of Bee's accident my mind went to Omz's accident, over and over. I just had to ask the difficult question.

With an anxious sigh I proceeded, "Do you think someone killed Omz and tried to kill Bee?"

Dad turned his head in shock and with a serious look answered, "It had entered my mind."

Avoiding any more conversation on this thought, he continued talking about the history of the family.

"Your mother and I decided to relocate to the coach house and move into the larger one later. That way Pa wouldn't have to decide what he wanted to keep or get rid off. It seemed easier that way. "

"I wondered why we suddenly changed gears instead of moving into the big house," I responded.

"Your Pa seemed so disoriented and preoccupied after the death of Omz." Dad was glad I remembered so much about her even though it had been a few years.

CHAPTER 19

The Connection

At this point, Dad said, they could not afford the big house, although the electricity was left on. Pa had paid for the electricity in advance for up to two years. He wanted it left on for some mysterious reason. Dad's search was over, until now of course. The mansion would not be torn down because of our findings. Dad needed to go back to work to make some money for the accumulating bills. I immediately wondered, how was he going to investigate this place if he went back to work?

The night was wearing on and we had done much talking, but there was still a lot to be discovered. This room had to be connected to the storage room somehow. Everything was laid out so carefully and it seemed with purpose. Where would we start?

"Let's use all the clues we found in the past, and see what we come up with," Dad said.

There was no keyhole that we could see, and there was no nail sticking out of the wall. There could be a protruding stone that we could push, but the place was made of rough stone. How would we find it? There was no barrel in sight, but ... I did see that misplaced looking crate. The one in the storage room moved, so maybe... this one would too.

Dad scrutinized every inch of the wooden, over-sized box.

He knocked on it and pushed it. Oddly enough, it too would not be moved, but had a hollow sound. I decided to try to lift the top, and yes it lifted easily, just as it was made to. It was empty inside, but, by this time, we knew better than to take for granted what we saw with our eyes.

There was a small knot hole in a wooden base. It did not look like it was there by chance. Dad reached in with his finger and pulled. The floor came up.

It was my cue to attach my pouch to my belt and take my box. Dad had the key and we took one of the old dusty lanterns. Dad turned the other two off and we took the chair away from the door leading to the stair to the study. Everything looked as we left it.

There were steep stairs going down from the bottom of the huge old crate. One leg at a time over the edge and Dad went first, down into the unknown. After handing Dad the lantern I followed and let the top close above me when I was low enough. I tried to lift it again and it rose effortlessly over my head. *Good,* I thought to myself. We could always return the same way.

It would have been dark, but the lantern guided our every step safely, all the while making huge creepy shadows on the walls. This was a nicely made stairway not cut in the stone like some of the others, but instead made of wood.

I told Dad how we should check the compass some time and make a visual map of all the passageways. He agreed as he kept forging ahead.

My excitement intensified as I wondered what we would find next. Every time I had been down here it was one discovery after another. This time it would be with Dad. We had shared a lot of things but never this kind of adventure and a secret so important. The stairs ended and turned into a boardwalk kind of path. We scanned the walls carefully for anything unusual but found nothing.

Suddenly some lights went on. It shocked us and caused our hearts to race.

"Who did that?" I asked, and, of course Dad didn't know.

We could see better because of the electric light, but left our lantern on. The light might be diminished as quickly as it was turned on.

We saw a door at the end of our walkway.

" I can't believe this, it is too easy and there is a doorknob."

All we could do was try it and see what would happen. First, we checked under our feet to see if the floor was moveable. With the boards, it was difficult to tell. They felt tight when we tried to lift them. We stomped hard, but as quietly as possible and they sounded the same as all the rest. Okay we were ready and had exhausted our options.

"Stay close Josh."

" I will, don't worry."

He turned the doorknob and nothing happened.

I heard a whispered, "Come on," from Dad.

It turns but nothing happens. What is going on?

"Let me try," I pleaded.

Dad let me squeeze by him. He took the lantern, and I grabbed the doorknob, turning it and then without letting go, pushed it down.

"Voila!" It unlocked.

Dad looked amazed, and he could tell I was starting to think like the designer of this place.

I pulled the door towards me, and heard the loudest scream. It was somehow familiar.

When the lantern lit the room, I could see why.

Dad demanded: "Mac ...and Mark ... What are you doing here? Did anyone see you?"

" No, no, no one saw us I promise."

Mac continued, "I tried to get a hold of you on your phone, but no one answered. Then I heard about the accident and the witness and I got scared that something happened to you. I tried to call your house and no one answered."

"Did you leave a message?" Dad interjected.

Mac retorted, "No I didn't want to get anyone into trouble, so I hung up!"

"Yeah, so she came over to my place and said I had to come find you, and that you might be in big . . . trouble."

Looking at Dad, Mark said, "I guess you're not, eh?"

"Okay, let's settle down and keep our wits about us, shall we," he said sounding like my Dad again.

Scratching his head Dad continued, "Josh do you realize we have found the passage to the storage room?"

It hadn't dawned on me until that moment. My friends' appearance put everything else on the back burner.

"Yes, all right," as I high-fived Dad!

The door led straight into the storage room and before us stood the four old crates we had found earlier. Before we closed the door, we checked to see if we could open and close it from the other side.

There wasn't one knob, but three knobs in a row, looking like coat hangers. Why hadn't I noticed them before? They seemed to have no purpose other than to hang things on.

Let's see, everything in here works like some mechanical genius has created it. I said, "The barrel turns and gets pushed down. Close the door and let's try it."

"Yes, let's try it, shall we?" Dad suggested.

I went over and turned the barrel and pushed it down to the ground. No, nothing happened.

"Okay how about the barrel marked, 'gun powder'?" Mac retorted in a commanding tone, not to be out done.

"We can try it!" said Dad.

"Will it blow up?"

"No, but let's have a good look at it first. The lid came off so easily and yet it has good threads on it, so it should close tightly."

Mac and Mark stood by, mesmerized by our fervor in finding out how to close the door.

"I am going to try to screw it on the way it looks like it should be," Dad muttered as he set the lid back into place.

Dad felt to see if the lid felt tight so the gunpowder wouldn't spill all over the stone floor. He found the threads interlocked nicely as it turned the lid, so he was sure it was making a good seal.

Suddenly, the seal felt stripped and we all watched as the lid turned too easily.

The door closed!

"Well I have never," were the words out of Dad's mouth.

It worked just as it should with the lid on properly.

Mark was beside himself. This was all new to him and he hadn't had time to anticipate an adventure around every corner. We stared at him as he went on and on about how neat this was, until Dad spoke up.

We then had a meeting on the importance of telling no one what we had found. I would show Mark and Mac the other tunnel at another time.

"So, it was you who put the light on, right?" I questioned Mac with an intensity she was not used to hearing from me.

She countered, "It also operates the light in the tunnel to the large cave and that is cool. We can always tell if someone is coming down with the light on."

"That is good to know," Dad added.

"I realized we had missed something very important," Dad said, after taking a moment to go over everything in his head.

"Mac, did you say there was a witness?"

Mark joined in, "Yes a witness came forward! The person said he was off in the darkness, where there were no streetlights."

Mac took over telling us the details she learned from her Dad, Barry, a police officer.

The witness was jogging a short distance behind the truck and the driver of the truck would not have seen him. He saw the truck stopped and pointing in the wrong direction, near the driveway light, facing your driveway. When it saw the headlights of an approaching car, with its right signal on, it started up and rammed full-speed ahead straight into the approaching vehicle.

He thought the person inside the car was a goner because the truck headed right for the driver's side. The truck sped away at top speed. The witness ran home just across the street to call 911. On quickly returning, he saw an ambulance at the scene, so he thought he would not be needed as assistance had arrived so quickly. The ambulance arrived, completely by chance, returning from the last call.

The witness also reported that, from where he was, the truck looked new. When the witness got back home he called in a report to the police, who went out to investigate.

That bit of news frightened us all and we knew that everyone was now in danger.

"Mac, you and Mark will not be allowed back down here anymore. Your families could be in great danger if anyone finds out you know about this place. We know we are in danger and will try to figure out how to stay safe. You should get back now as your parents will be wondering where you are and we don't want to stir up suspicion. If you find you are in trouble please go to Barry. He will help you. We have stuff to do back home too."

"You sure do, your place is a mess," Mac exclaimed!

"And how do you know that," asked Dad?

"We stopped by your place and went inside when no one answered. I know where the key is in case the door is locked. I was shocked that it was. We had a look around and your room, and saw that it was a total disaster. You have got to clean it up before Bee and your mom get home tomorrow, or…is it today? They are coming home soon, aren't they?"

"I sure hope so although I don't know if they will be safe here," Dad almost choked as he said the words.

"For now, no one comes back here until we find out what to do next—do you all hear me?" insisted Dad.

"Yes sir!" came out in unison, sounding like an unrehearsed, out of beat, choir. Dad gave orders not to discuss anything inside our house, as it might be bugged. I would have to check it out and have it swept. He said our life was going to depend on everyone working together.

"We understand," said Mark.

Mac nodded her head in agreement.

"Leave the lantern and the box here, Josh. We'll put it in the back room next time. I think it is safer here than at our place. You two can leave by the gazebo this time, and Josh and I will wait until you and Mark have gone before we come out. Be careful."

Dad agreed that I should put the tape on the wall so we could find the door from both directions. We did this right away. Mac and

Mark took note of where the tape was placed.

"That will be much easier than counting the stairs!" Marc exclaimed.

We left the box from my room in the storage room, but I took the tape. Dad waited for the door to close behind us. Dad and I once again took note of that, not-so-obvious place, where we had shown Marc and Mac the placement of the tape. We placed the tape on the opposite side of the pressure point. If you knew it was there you could find it, but we were sure no one else would spot it.

We made our way up the stairs, waiting at the top while we pulled the chain to turn the light off below. It was now early morning and we knew that we had to get some sleep before Mom got home. We decided to talk on the drive to the hospital.

Dad thought maybe Bee and Mom should go on a little holiday to Grammy and Grammpy's farm, in Pennsylvania Amish country.

CHAPTER 20

Bee Comes Home

As our minds had difficulty shutting down to sleep, our alarms woke us much too early. Dad slept in my double bed with me as his was torn apart. I think it was easier for both of us knowing we were together and safe. Dad made a coffee and I had a hot chocolate. We had some toast and peanut butter. I cleaned up the dishes, and noticed Mom's delicious dessert still on the counter, so I put it in the fridge.

I realized life could change so very quickly, without warning.

Dad started on his room. I joined him as soon as I could and we set up the dressers, chairs and put the drawers back in their place. He had already made the bed and started sorting the clothes, deciding what should go in each drawer. It wouldn't be perfect, but certainly not as upsetting as it previously appeared. We had it all put away and I think Mom wouldn't realize until she was looking for something.

We had done a good job and were pleased with ourselves.

At 9 a.m. Dad called the hospital to talk to Mom. She had also had a long night with all the noise and the nurses checking in on Bee, but was so happy to hear from us.

The police had already been there to see if Bee could give a description of the truck. She tried but couldn't remember any other details. She remembered the lights turning on in front of her and thinking she had to turn out of the way. The officer said that was what had saved her life. It looked like the truck had a large metal piece on the front of it. It had to be rusty as some of the rust was on Bee's car where it was hit. That didn't add up with an eyewitness report, which said it looked like a new vehicle from the back.

Dad said he would be happy to pick her and Bee up as soon as possible and asked about Bee's release.

Dr. Schultz would be in shortly and sign her out as well as give them a report regarding the test results.

Dad told her we were on our way.

We talked about Dad's plan.

Bee and Mom would be sent to Mom's parent's farm. The Amish community was a tight-knit one, and strangers were easily recognized. Our family was known in this little community as Mom grew up there and we spent many summers with Grammy and Grammpy.

I asked, "What are we going to do, Dad?"

He said we would plan a road trip, and I was shocked!

"Not us. Just our car with Mom and Bee."

Dad said this, calming me down after his bizarre statement.

"Oh, and how is that going to work?" I asked.

We needed some time to do some uninterrupted investigating. We were going to get some travel brochures from the Canadian Automobile Association this morning as well as insurance for all of us. Then we would talk to some people and let them know the family was going away for a while on a cross-country trip. We would start with Dr. Schultz and so on. We would let as many as possible know about our trip. We could stop in at Mark's and Mac's and let them know personally.

I suggested to Dad, "You and I will get supplies and all we can think of that we need and take them down below. I was thinking we should take that little bar fridge that Pa has in the shed behind the carriage house."

"You know that composting toilet Pa has in there too? It might be useful, Dad."

"I am starting to wonder if he bought all that stuff for a purpose. I don't know what happened but I wish he had told me what was going on. I'm sure I could have been some help to him."

"So Dad, I was thinking about just that. I think we should tell Mom and Bee what we know and discovered, and how safe we will be while we are searching for clues down there."

"For such a young man you have figured out how to learn from watching others make mistakes. I've noticed you learn quickly to follow patterns too."

He chuckled as he said the latter.

"My teacher last year said I was a genius at solving problems, didn't he?"

We were having a good time and actually having conversation, man to man. I was enjoying this every bit as much as Dad. We continued to make our concrete plans while in the car driving to the hospital.

We both decided we would see how Bee felt, and give her a day or two before they would leave. We would drive the car across the US border and store it in a friend's garage.

We had connections to drivers that chauffeured the Amish long distances, as they could not drive themselves. The driver was always an impeccably trust-worthy person. The Amish parents had no hesitation in sending their unmarried young people with this person, as they traveled great distances. Our ladies would get a ride with one of them from Buffalo to Lancaster. Grammpy would pick them up from there in his horse and buggy. They would be disguised enough once they changed into the Amish clothing Grammy kept for them.

"I think we should show the girls around so they can see for themselves that we will be safe if no one tells our secret. They wouldn't believe it unless they see it with their own eyes."

I agreed with Dad and thought it was a good idea. We completed our plans shortly after we went by Queenston Heights, the home of Brock's Monument.

Tourists were already starting to fill the Niagara parking lot and the buses caused a little traffic jam. The sun shone brightly and the heat of it would soon make everyone edgy and impatient.

The hospital parking lot was busy and it took us a while to find a spot. Dad wanted to park close to the entrance, as we didn't know what shape Bee would be in. There was an inexpensive parking lot across the street but the matter of saving money didn't come into play today.

Nearing Bee's room, I hoped she was feeling better. She could be a pain to everyone around, if she was under the weather. That was from a younger brother's perspective of course.

Yes, she was dressed and sitting on the bed waiting, her favorite coffee in her hand, a French vanilla. Around the top of her mouth a nice dirty white ring of foam.

"Clean up, Sis, you are going home."

"What do you mean? I'm clean."

Mom passed her a napkin, telling her I meant her mouth as she gave me a "*Stop...*" look. I knew that look, so I tried my best to cool it. Bee didn't need that big sister treatment quite yet.

Dad kissed Mom and then his daughter on the forehead. He did this in his usual gentle way and stroked the back of Bee's head.

"How are you feeling?" he asked.

"I feel good, Dad. I just want to get out of here, but the doctor hasn't been here yet."

Just then the doctor walked in, as though he was on cue in a written script.

"Well, I have checked all the test results and this is one ... lucky... girl. You have no internal injuries and other then being stiff and bruised you should be fine in a couple of days."

Mom let out a "Thank you, Lord."

Dad thanked John for being there for us, and for the good report.

As the doctor walked out we all looked at each other and couldn't help but laugh and make happy gestures. You know—"high fives", "yippee" and "awesome"!

All those signs showed how happy we were.

Dad left the room for a few minutes and waited before we stopped at the nurses' station for some prescribed Tylenol. It really felt like we were going home as we made our getaway to the nearest elevator, and pushed the button.

On the way down our family was alone and Dad told us we had to talk before we got home. It had to be a secret and no one could know.

The elevator stopped and a man got in. We said no more, until we exited on the main floor. The man followed us until Dad steered Bee into the gift shop.

We followed of course.

"Do you need anything?" he asked.

"No I don't think so Dad," she replied.

I knew what Dad was doing and why.

We slowly made our way out of the shop and through the doors to the outside. Bee breathed a big sigh of relief as she got her first gasps of that fresh morning air.

Nearing our vehicle, we noticed a familiar looking man just sitting in his car.

He was parked just across from us and I could see Dad getting the furrowed brow again. It looked as if he was the same man in the elevator with us.

I asked Mom for a napkin out of the glove compartment and I knew I had a pen in the back pocket behind the driver's seat right in front of me.

Looking at the car, I jotted down the license plate number as well as the car's make and colour. We would give that to Mac's dad, Barry, a police officer who could do a trace on it.

Dad stalled for a while but the guy didn't seem to move. As Dad started our car to pull out, the other man also started his. This was weird! We had to stop to pay money at the parking lot exit, so Dad decided to see if he could get change from the guy behind us. As he stepped out, to approach him, the guy stepped on the gas pedal, drove around us and went through the gate, breaking it. He must have smashed something on his vehicle too. Stepping back into our car quickly Dad said, "Well I guess he didn't want to talk to me did he? Josh did you get the info?"

"Yep, I did."

Dad looked at the rear-view mirror and nodded in approval at what he saw. Mom and Bee were frightened and wondered what that was all about. Dad said we would call Mac's dad, Barry, and give him the details later. We needed a serious family talk.

After stopping at the CAA for all kinds of maps and info, the girls were totally confused. The next stop was the Old Queen's Coach Restaurant. It was an unassuming place with great history, friendly waitresses and good food. The breakfasts were enough to keep you going most of the day. We frequented it many times with Pa and Omz and were told about the carriages that stopped there on the way from Niagara Falls to Queenston and Niagara-on-the-Lake.

We grabbed a corner booth and Bee and I sat on one side as Mom and Dad sat on the other.

Dad took Mom's hand from her lap, her face inquiring as she looked into his eyes. Dad's eyes spoke volumes. They were truly the window to his thoughts and emotions and Mom was good at discerning his mood.

Dad started by telling them about the witness and what the police knew. He told about their room being torn apart. And he was having the house swept clean this afternoon and knew it could be bugged again.

Before we went any further, Bee got teary eyed and said, "Do you mean someone was really trying to kill me…? Why…?"

Dad said we didn't know yet but we were on our way to finding out, and we had to be very casual about it while we spoke.

She handled it well and I patted her arm, to let her know we were there for her. It must have been such a shock to her finding out someone wanted her dead. She was in such a fragile state right now and would have to gather all within her to be brave.

Dad said he had a plan and explained it.

Bee didn't like leaving her work and friends. She would have to have a letter from Dr. Schultz sent to the lodge to explain her absence. He also insisted that she should contact many friends and to tell them she would be on a road trip without data.

She did not like the thoughts of going to Amish country and knew she would be known as, "Die Englishe."

Dad convinced her she would be safe there with her mother until they got to the bottom of the mystery.

We had our coffee, hot chocolate and ordered breakfast from a friendly waitress who stayed to chat. She asked if we heard about the guy who tried to kill that young girl last night, but wasn't successful! She went on about how terrible this world has gotten and how you have to watch your back. We agreed, and her co-worker brought our breakfasts.

By the time they left Bee knew she had to leave. The waitress's timely exhortation of Bee's accident made her realize she was not safe anymore.

We told them a little of what we found, and they could see it tonight if they were up to it. We would always keep all windows and doors locked, and the alarms on even when we were home. We needed to be careful. We should tell our friends and pave the way for our road trip.

"Remember we are all supposed to be going together, right?" Dad reminded all of us.

"The plan is to cross over the border at the Rainbow Bridge in town with you and get to Jake's place within twenty minutes. The bikes on the bike rack will be our way home. The car will be safely stored in the garage out of sight. We will see you off first and then Josh and I can bike back and be inconspicuous. We will even go the back way if we have to do so."

"Are you sure you are going to be alright? And how will we know?" Mom asked.

We would tell them about our communication plan later.

"Do you think you will be able to find the answers soon?" Mom worried.

Dad spoke, with confidence in his voice. "I hope so, it would be nice to have this whole thing behind us. I also think it will help us to find out what happened to Pa."

We paid our bill and walked to our car, checking out all the other vehicles and being much more aware than we had been before. On the way home, we stopped at Mac's place, to talk to her dad, Barry, as it was his day off. We were close to Mac's family and Dad jogged with Barry, so we knew his schedule. They welcomed us in and offered us a coffee. Mom and Bee sat down as the girls' chatting session began.

Mac gave me the eye and I followed her to their sunroom. Dad and Barry were in the office.

"Mac do you know someone was following us today?"

"No."

"Yes, right from inside the elevator to the parking lot," I added.

I told her all about it and that she would need to be a go-between, for Mom, Bee and us. They would have her number and she would have Grammy's outside phone number. Mac would need to be patient as it took time for anyone to reach the phone when it rang. She would drop off the messages at the cemetery at Great-Opa and Oma's graves.

Great-Opa had a large monument that Pa erected. He even exhumed the bodies to put them in a special spot at the head of the little cemetery. It was kept clean by a tap continuously running water down the three-foot wide trough. Omz had her own monument, with the same design of the basket and flowers as Great-Opa and Oma's which were together.

I imagined that he had a circulating pump built into it, and it would bring the water back up and recycle it. The trough was about five feet long. It was beautiful, as well as unique.

There was a great hiding spot for letters in the basket of flowers carved from the granite. I could never figure out why the water ran beside the flowers instead of on the basket. I would fix that, one day. I figured it was just a matter of carefully adjusting the spout.

Mac was to use the spot under the roses where the carved, broad leaves hung over the basket. There was enough room under them for good size letters. She would put the messages in zip locked bags with a stone so they didn't get wet or float away.

She agreed and I told her we were going to find some answers this time, but only when Mom and Bee were safe. She had to be careful as we realized our place was being watched. Someone might want to snoop if we were gone. I am sure Barry would have patrol cars pass in and out of the driveway daily, but we could not be too careful. If something did not feel right we decided we would ask for our "special password." That would verify who we were.

I heard Dad as he told Barry he would be by later for the information, and that he couldn't call until this evening after he knew the house had been "swept" for listening devices. He wanted to get Bee home to rest a bit, as she would be feeling her aching muscles more now than earlier.

We were on our way and Dad said he would take me over to Mark's place now. He did not want us wandering about in the neighbourhood, being made so vulnerable at this time. We stopped across the road at Mark's place. Mark had moved in as a young boy and we have been good buddies ever since. We played at school and each time I visited Pa and Omz. My feelings were mixed at telling him a lie about where we would be. He was a very good friend. His hair, a medium brown, was worn very short and it accentuated his dark brown eyes. He was athletic in all ways. We were opposites in all ways except in height and the way our minds worked and stayed in sync.

I knocked on the door and Mark answered. I motioned for him to come outside, as he had a distant relative living with him, who I did not like. We talked quietly and I asked him to be on call if Mac needed him to do anything. We were going away and needed him to be there for Mac.

"Of course," he agreed. "You can count on me."

No one could know, it was top secret, I said, and our lives depended on it.

He nodded his head and said, "Good luck, buddy." I thanked him, and left.

Getting back into the car I wondered, did anyone ever check this relative of Mark's out?

"Dad can you check out this new guy at Mark's place?

"Sure what's his name, but why?" Dad asked.

"I just have a sense about him, and he is always sneaking around and shows up everywhere. He seems to be asking a lot of questions that don't concern him and Mark thinks he should get a job."

"Well," with a chuckle Dad suggested, " We can't check on him for having no job, but if he is suspicious it is as good a reason as any, especially in our situation. Write his name down for me and I will take it over to Barry later when I go to see him."

"Okay," I answered.

We were finally home again and Dad apologized to Bee for taking the long way. She replied that she understood. We all got in the house and Mom went straight to her room. It looked good, but we knew she would be frustrated when she had to pack.

She said she would help Bee after she did her packing. Bee could take a rest first. She was starting to get very sore now, which we suspected would happen. Her chest was bruised as well as her legs. Mom gave her some medication, and a glass of water to help her soreness.

Dad and I packed our bags too, including all those things that we thought we would need for our stay.

There was a knock on the door and Dad answered, while we all held our breath and ran to see who it might be. It was an old buddy from the police station who came to "sweep" the place. He didn't say what he was doing but quietly walked through all the rooms with a detector of some kind.

As he found the listening devices he took them, disarmed them and put them in his bag.

The kitchen had only one near the hood fan, which was always on. Thank goodness! The bathroom had one, and Mom and Dad's bedroom had one. The living room had two. Who would put one in the bathroom? That was just gross.

He then took out another detector and started checking at the door, walking all around each room along the wall. We were clear. He said not to let anyone in who we did not know and not to bring anything home that we did not pack ourselves. That meant groceries, clothes from the cleaners, knapsacks, work clothes, gifts, you name it. Take-out food, and our friends, he added just to stress the point. Dad thanked him for a job well done and walked him to the door. I could tell Bee was more shaken up than she was letting on.

As soon as Dad left she said, "This is not going away is it?" She was shaking. I said, "Bee sit down, I know you are scared but you are going to be fine."

I put my arms around her in a brotherly fashion so she could relax. She took a deep breath and I told her I was proud of how she was doing. I didn't know if I could have done as well. She got all weepy just as Dad came back in.

"Hey what's going on?"

"Oh my little brother was just being so sweet it made me cry," she said.

"Well Josh, the talents you have been hiding are being exposed by the minute."

"Yes, he is becoming like a big brother, isn't he?"

It was enough to make me blush; thank goodness Mom came in to rescue me.

"I have finished my packing and I can help you, Bee."

"I'll be right there," she said as she turned to go to her room, after giving me a "thank you" smirk.

"Keep all the blinds down!" Dad shouted.

We were not used to living such paranoid lives, but yes it was necessary for a while.

Bee was resting after Mom had helped her to quicken her packing job. Dad and I were already packed, waiting to take the girls on the tour of our newfound secrets.

We were also discussing the entrance we should take the girls to. The gazebo had to be crawled into. Then they had to use the stairs, which were well lit.

The slide might be too rough with that abrupt stop, but was the fastest way. The study was a sophisticated way with its hidden doors, but had many steps. It looked like Bee would be able to make the steps. She was strong, as long as she wasn't too sore.

"We will see. Maybe you can take Mom one way, and I will go the other with Bee," Dad suggested.

"Hey, that sounds like fun, Dad."

We would have to wait until they are feeling ready. The sooner they were out of here, the better we would feel for their safety.

Bee and Mom took a while to discuss one more outfit which Bee wanted take with her. It didn't really seem like a holiday although they should treat it like one. Never mind the fact that they would look so different than their Amish family.

Dad told me he had made all the phone calls to Buffalo, where we were leaving our car and Bee and Mom were connecting with their Amish ride. He also left a message for his in-laws and did it all from the hospital. This way the calls could not be traced to him, or his family. He was aware of his surroundings and felt no one could hear him. Then we quietly waited until the ladies were ready.

Bee said, “Do I have to change or something?”

Dad and I smirked, and spoke in unison, “Only if you want to.”

“Okay, okay, I get it, the answer is no.” She retorted.

I had my pouch and Dad had the key. We each had our flashlights, but were not using them until we were out of sight. Dad was going first with Bee. Mom and I would wait and leave from the back door and go down the side ravine via the gorge and the gazebo.

Mom was to make sure the alarm was set and the door was locked. The girls were in for the treat of their lives. I'll bet they never experienced anything like this before. I was so excited to show them about the house.

Dad and Bee left from the side door and circled around the back of the house towards the old mansion. Bee was staying close behind him.

“Watch your step and don't trip,” Dad whispered.

They made it to the old home and went in through the double doors. The moon was fading, but still gave enough light, so they could find their way around. Dad went to the bookcase entrance of the study. Even Bee knew of it and was not impressed.

They slipped in and closed the door. It was dark until Dad switched on his flashlight.

He shone it towards the old cabinet and opened the drawer as before. He pulled the lever inside at the back of the drawer and the cabinet opened.

Now Bee was impressed.

“Are you sure we should go in there?” she whispered.

“Come on,” said Dad as he pulled her hand. He asked her to stand behind him and he opened the hatch with his key. The hatch lifted and, with his flashlight, he let Bee down first.

The hatch closed and they followed the long twisting tunnel to the other door. Bee was so intrigued that she forgot about her pain.

With the flashlight beam illuminating the door, Dad again opened it and they entered the room as before. This time to Bee's surprise they had company. It was Mom and Josh!

Bee was ecstatic at what she had just experienced and Mom was wondering how in the world we found this place. We explained it was only days ago and it was just last night that Dad found the study stairway.

I explained that there was a lot more to see and tunnels even went to the edge of the cliff, far down on the rock face. We were now just figuring this place out, and how to get here, so we should be able to uncover some secrets, given more time.

We went into the storage room via the tunnel and we showed them all the plans we had to study. There were drawings that could tell us something. There was my box that had sat on my dresser all those years, and I wasn't aware that these were even real pictures. They just looked like a design of some kind to me. Dad and I were going to shack up down here and make ourselves comfortable, so we could find the answers to Pa's secret.

As we walked back to the living cave we talked freely, and answered questions. We helped Bee with those steep stairs once again and it felt good to be together in our hideaway.

"We told you because Josh realized that, if Pa would have confided in his family, he might have been with us today and Bee would not have been in this accident, if you can call it that," Dad said.

"We want you to be informed and be aware of circumstances in your lives, as well as the people around you. You can see if this is kept a secret we are totally safe. No one must know until we find the answers. You should be safe too, but if something does go wrong, you could come back, and you both know how to access this place."

"But I don't have a key!" Bee exclaimed.

"That is true but your mother knows how to get in without one. Can you bend very low?" Dad asked.

"Yes, I can, I think," was her reply as Bee bent over.

"Then we might try to show you... we will see," Dad said very calmly.

He showed them where we left the marking, telling them that the light went on if you pulled the chain on top.

"Josh did not use the light today, as you noticed, and you could still see the tape with his flash light. Remember the tape is directly opposite of the marker. Don't be afraid to lean on the marker with your body and the door will open. Once inside, if you get no further, the door will close and you will be very safe. The door closes automatically, as soon as you step in. We would find you, if you came to this room. We will have more supplies in just a short while."

Josh also told the girls about the water under the crate, the Coleman, paper and pencils, typewriter, gunpowder and more, and how to access all of them. Dad hoped they could remember it all.

"Okay, okay, I think I feel confident about getting in now," stated Bee.

"Oh," Josh said, "there is a fast way down here from the side parlor."

We thought it was too rough for you today as it is a slide, but the floor falls down from under you."

We wanted to show them the slide for easy access, so we decided to just tell Bee about the stairs outside this door that went straight up to under the gazebo, as well as down towards the cliff, and that they would be hers to discover another time. She didn't like the idea of missing anything.

As we made our way back to our "living room", Dad added, "There are two boards loose beside the stairs on the gorge side."

It made a safe escape as the door with hinges and a latch on the riverside opened to the eroded edge of the gazebo, and to death. *Always put the boards back.* It was the rule. We told them with great emphasis. *Never leave from behind the steps without checking if someone is there.* We were trying to give them all the information that we could.

Bee said she would remember and so did Mom, as they both started to check out our cozy room now that we were back. We all agreed it was pretty charming although rustic, in its furnishings.

"Well we had better get you back so you can rest. You both have a big day tomorrow and so do we," Dad suggested.

With that, we took one more look and Mom noticed Pa's clock.

"I would love to hear that clock chime once more," Mom said sentimentally.

I told her the chimes were turned off but I could put it on if she liked.

"The chimes will sound echoed down here and it will be a nice effect!" I enthusiastically encouraged.

"Yes it would be so wonderful," Mom replied.

I bent to pick it up and clicked the pin to the chime position. I also moved the hands to the hour mark so we could enjoy the chimes. One minute to go. Another minute passed and there was a dull clang. I wondered what that was? What a disappointment, and we all moaned. I picked the heavy clock up once more, turning it over and looked in the little door at the back. It looked intricate with all its small wheels. I took my flashlight, and there, stuck in one chamber, was a metal object.

Dad came over to have a look and I quickly pulled out a tweezers, from my pouch and passed it to Dad.

"Here you go Dad."

He pulled just a little and out came ... a key? Immediately his hands dug in his pocket and pulled out his key.

Comparing the two he proclaimed, "They are the same. How do you like that?"

"Can we have one Dad?" asked Bee.

"Yes I think that will work but you cannot lose it."

"We won't right, Mom?"

Mom said she would wear it around her neck on a heavy chain, and no one would see it, especially with the clothes they would be wearing. We tried it on the doors as we left and it worked. There was always two of everything.

Of course, we all got the privilege of hearing Pa's old clock chime once more, and I was right. It sounded wonderful in our cave. The chimes rang out as never before.

Mom and Dad got a little teary eyed but enjoyed the sound of the old clock's chimes once more. What a sound!

Going up the stairs, Bee was getting tired and we promised it would not be much longer. She used her key to get up through the hatch to the small space behind the study. It was crowded standing on the little slip of wood floor while we put the hatch down again. Mom took the key and put it into the deepest pocket of her slim jeans. We pointed out that the study was on the other side of this wall. We explained how you had to pull this little metal lever for the hutch and wall to move so Mom could see it too. Dad showed Mom and she pulled it. The hutch moved and we were in the study again.

I reminded them of the slide and told them it was just on the other side of this wall in a hall that no one knew about. There was a door in the wall on the other side, from the side room facing the gazebo. I found it many years ago, as a child. I hid in there many times and no one could find me.

I looked for a door leading to Pa's study but never found one.

"Let's have a look at that wall again?" asked Dad.

We shone our lights and scanned it. I had learned from Dad that a flashlight would accent an area much more than full light.

"The only thing different that I can see is that the trim is crooked where it should be straight," Dad reported.

He went over to see if it was loose and if he could straighten it. As he pushed it down into place the wall opened.

"There we go, Son, and ladies of course," as he gestured with his hand to let them by.

He was quite pleased with himself and impressed Mom and Bee even more.

I warned them regarding the nail while assuring them that they wouldn't get hurt. It was a shock the first time as we were unsuspecting.

I couldn't believe we now had the second door into the study. Dad and I had such a satisfied look on our faces.

"Well we will go first and you and Mom can come after us," I told Dad.

"Bee do you have your key for the house with you?" Mom asked.

She did and we were off. We edged our way down to the ravine and snuck back into the house by the side door. The alarms were still set and we were in the clear. We sat and waited for Mom and Dad. It seemed to take so long.

What were they doing? I would have to go look for them soon. Finally we heard them at the side door. "Where were you?" I demanded.

"A car had pulled onto our driveway and just sat there. We couldn't get out of the house with those lights on the mansion," Dad replied.

"What next?" we all thought.

"Oh, maybe it was Barry with some news, I will call him." Dad rubbed his chin.

Barry answered immediately and verified that he had sat on our drive way for a long time, pondering. It was so dark and he didn't know if we were sleeping. He said he would be right over if that was okay.

The girls went to get ready for bed and I waited with Dad.

When he arrived, Barry had some notes in his hands.

CHAPTER 21

The Suit

As Barry handed me the papers he affirmed, "You know I usually don't do this but someone tried to kill your daughter."

I started to read. The car at the hospital belonged to a Mr. Sims, but the vehicle was stolen a couple of days ago.

"Can I get a description of the guy from you? You said he was on the elevator with the family?" he inquired as he looked at Dad and I.

I spoke up spontaneously, "Let's see, he wore a blue suit, and had dress shoes on, and his hair looked very greasy."

Just then Bee and Mom appeared, looking cozy in their robes. They came in for a drink before turning in for the night.

"Barry asked them, "Can you describe this man on the elevator?"

Bee started with, "Yes, he had on an expensive after shave lotion for men."

Mom interjected, "What was it . . . yes, 'Straight to Heaven,' by Kilian and it goes for about $225.00."

Dad and I looked surprised, as Bee came out with, "His suit was Brooks Brothers and it goes for around $14,000.00 and ... his shoes were Tanino Crisci's Lilian Shoes and they only go for..."

Mom stammered a little and tried to get the words before Bee, "Ah . . . Ah . . . Ah . . . "

" . . . $1,250.00!" Bee blurted out as they were challenged to play their game.

Barry asked if they were, " . . . for real." We knew they were and made quite a display of it at times, but Bee had gotten very, very good. We just didn't think they were so aware of their surroundings with Bee's accident and all.

Could they describe his face was his next question, as he looked at Bee.

"He had some scars on his face from acne and used too much hair product. It looked way too greasy. He also wore a, 'George' shirt, which I found to be a strange combination. Nothing against Walmart but not combined with Brooks Brothers. He had to be a 'wannabe.' He also sported a ring on his wedding finger that had a 'G' on it. It was black onyx and gold."

Bee added, " His nose had a small scar on the...left side. He also had a muddy complexion."

"You ladies are fabulous. Thank you very much. This guy will be so easy to find."

Barry continued, "Now about the other matter, we have not been able to catch him with a single thing yet, except he is known to deal in marijuana and other drugs and is being watched. Until he is caught we can do nothing. Since he lives so close to you we will put our feelers out, and keep a closer eye on him."

With that he said good night, and wished us a great time away.

"I'm sure it will do you all a lot of good."

Dad locked the door after putting the alarm on. He didn't realize we felt safe because he was home with us and not because of the alarm system.

CHAPTER 22

Leaving for Our Trip

Meeting at the breakfast table we chatted about our pretend family trip and even laughed as we described a few strange scenarios as to what could happen during it. One was sitting around a campfire at night enjoying our marshmallows when a huge bear got Bee because she was too scared and frozen to run away. Of course I knew I would get the backlash of that story when I was least expecting it. After all, we were siblings.

Early in the morning we got loaded up, and put the bikes on the rack. Of course Dad and I didn't really take a lot. We just took only enough to fit into our bike packs for our ride home. Dad made a point of asking God to watch over his family as they were once again separated. It touched us all and Mom pulled out her tissue to regain her composure.

I watched the road and looked at all the areas that I knew we would pass riding our bikes back. It looked like a warm day and Dad and I would enjoy our return trip.

It was a bittersweet good-bye, as we would miss the girls, but knew they were safe on the farm, at least for a little while. Mom dreaded leaving Dad so soon after he had returned home.

Moms always seem to sacrifice where their families are concerned. I could see it took everything within her to leave us behind.

Our car was tucked away in the garage and Mom and Bee had

their luggage in the Amish transit car. It was black and plain but roomy. The driver was a Mennonite gentleman from Lancaster. He wore his straw hat and black suit with humility. Belonging to a new order Amish sect, he owned the car he was driving.

We hugged our ladies one last time and they were off. We stood there and waved until they were out of sight.

"Do you think they will be safe, Dad?"

"I hope so," he replied with his brow furrowed.

CHAPTER 23

Transported Back in Time

Mom and Bee settled in and Mom made some small talk with the Amish gentleman. He was a family man with 13 children.

Bee kept trying to look past his beard to see his face and just how old he really was. He had nice skin, and no wrinkles from what she could see. The beard and straw hat hid so much of his face. His hair was cut in a bowl shape and his black homemade suit gave him no personality, although his blue shirt popped from behind it.

The car was not air-conditioned and the girls felt hot and sticky. There would be another five hours of this torture, as Mr. Stolzfus was not going to break any speed limits.

Mom knew enough to pack a lunch, as they would only stop for the bathroom a couple of times.

Bee looked at her mom longingly as they passed a coffee shop along the highway. Mom just gave a slight shake of her head which meant a loud, "No and don't ask."

Bee read a book for the rest of her trip as she restlessly moved her aching body from one position to the next. By this time her bruises would be showing and her muscles would be stiffening and sore from the accident. Mom had packed her medication and Bee took it with the bottled water Mom thought to bring from home.

It was nearing supper time when they finally reached their destination. The many black horse-drawn carriages had modern slow-moving vehicle signs, or large strips of florescent tape on the back. This was so that they could be seen, and meant the vehicles were moving slowly—under 40-km an hour. The tape was for the Amish who were not permitted to have signs on their buggies as it was against their religion. The towns were trying to pass a law that they should all have lights on all their buggies. Bee had learned many things regarding the Amish as she was closely connected.

It seemed to take forever to get anywhere, as Bee was so accustomed to her fast pace of life.

Lancaster County now featured many new hotels, restaurants and shops. It was overrun with tourists and it seemed like the Amish were now squeezed in between the modern businesses.

This was strange as it was the Amish culture that drew all of these tourists to this area.

The vehicle turned down an old dirt road and the passengers' stomachs were fluttering. Not because of the road but because they knew they were almost at Grammy's and Grammpy's farm.

The large trees surrounded the old farmhouse, cradling it as if to protect it from the outside world. The large white barn stood close by. It housed the farm machinery and Grammpy's workshop. He manufactured parts for the farmers near and far. If they had need of something he could make it. He did it all using generators. They were not connected to any electric grid and loved it that way.

Grammy and Grammpy were uniquely different than the average Amish. They thought for themselves and only accepted what was permissible under the law and grace of the Bible, not the Bishop. They became people that lived by God's rules many years ago and made it through difficult times for that reason. They decided to live their life this way as they were used to it, and enjoyed their life style. Not because they felt under bondage from a bishop or group of people that would shun them.

There they were! The elderly couple was waiting on the front porch. They rose to their feet waving intently, as their family got out of the car. Bee ran over and gave them a big hug, as did Mom.

"Grammy, have you lost weight?" Mom asked.

"Maybe a little" Grammy replied looking at Grammpy.

The driver was thanked and paid for the lovely ride along with a basket of Grammy's homemade preserves. Glad they had finally arrived, they turned their attention back to the senior couple.

CHAPTER 24

Mom's Childhood Home

Grammpy took Bee's hand and led everyone into his humble home. Mom couldn't believe how it looked just as it had when she grew up there. The front room was a nice size with six windows to let in light. The gas lanterns were still in their strategic positions where they were used for reading and needlework. Grammy's old wooden rocker sat near a window on the far side of the room. Beside it lay her worn Bible with her reading glasses on top.

Grammpy had his own chair. It looked out the front window so he could see what was happening in the yard in front between the house and the barnyard.

Grammy asked, "You must be *gut* (good) and tired from your trip? Grammpy take their luggage to the rooms, please. Nissa will stay in her own room and Bee in the one across the hall."

"Nissa" was the short form for Nerissa, but Mom had been called this since she was a child.

The girls grabbed their own bags and refused to let the elderly man touch them. He chuckled a little in response to this. They must think of him as an old man!

Mom's room had a double bed. It had just one mattress, two pillows and the same hand-made quilt she used as a little girl. The same dresser stood against the long wall with the same small square mirror on the wall above it. She remembered not being able to see into it until she was seven years old. There was an old wooden chair in one corner and a row of hooks beside it. There hung the hangers that would be her closet. Mom hoped Bee would have enough room for her things.

CHAPTER 25

Surprise!

Bee walked into her room and gave a gasp.

"Wow," she said aloud. "I did not expect this."

Grammpy stood just behind Bee and asked, "Is it *gut*?"

"Like it, I love it!" she replied turning to give Grammpy a big hug.

Mom came out of her room after hearing the commotion and asked what was going on.

Bee exclaimed, "Come and see Mom, you won't believe it!"

Mom stepped into the room and her jaw dropped. The room had been painted in a lovely turquoise blue colour. The floor-length drapes on each of the two windows were in a black print with modern shapes of turquoise and white. There was a trendy headboard attached to a double bed with a box spring and high mattress. The luxurious bedding was covered with a hand-made quilt in an ultra-modern motif. The pillows adorned with various designs were extra fluffy and not only were there two, but five altogether.

An oversized armoire stood on one wall and would hold everything Bee had brought with her.

There was not only one chair, but also a lounger in the most delicious colour of turquoise. It sat beside a worn plank table that could double as a desk. There were hints of the prettiest soft pink throughout the materials and accents used in the room. The most beautiful piece of art in contrast to its old weathered frame hung on the wall over the bed. A lovely vase with sweet peas trailing from it stood on the dresser in front of a gigantic mirror.

On the floor on each side of the bed were large, soft pink fur carpets contrasting the wide old, worn floor planks. On entering the room, the soft bubble gum pink fur carpets called out to you.

It was not an Amish plain room at all but one that made a designer statement.

Grammpy began by telling them how Grammy got a friend from the Sights and Sound Theater in town to redo the room in a style that a modern young lady would appreciate. She knew that the family would be coming sometime this year and wanted it to be a place a young person would love.

Nissa and Bee were in awe and they walked around the room, touching everything. Bee opened a low door under the sloped ceiling, and yes, sure enough, the old attic access was still there. She loved that about this place and spent many hours playing there a child.

"Where is Grammy?" Bee asked.

Grammpy replied. "She stayed downstairs."

This was not like Grammy.

The girls went down to join Grammy and found her in her chair. After explaining how lovely they thought the room was and thanking her for such a lovely gift they heard about how Kelly got all the furniture and everything that was in the room, online for Grammy.

She took Kelly's word on what she should buy. Kelly asked the set designer at the theater as to how the room should look and what should go into it. The set designer was glad to help and even came down to have a look and put the final touches on the room. She told us how Kelly was such a good person and how she appreciated everything Kelly added.

"I will have to meet Kelly for myself and thank her in person."

Grammy's eyebrow rose, but before she could speak Grammpy came in and said we should have something to eat. The girls were famished and couldn't wait. Although they knew the way to the kitchen they followed the elderly couple.

While taking their place at the table Grammpy asked, "Well are you surprised about how *gut* the room turned out?"

Both reassured them that it was one of the nicest rooms they had ever seen.

Grammpy continued, "Just because we want to live a simple life doesn't mean we think it is wrong to live differently. We wanted to make sure you remembered that, Bee."

"Well you sure reminded us in a big way, Dat," Mom uttered her child-like name for Grammpy.

He smiled to hear his name spoken that way after such a long time.

Grammy had arranged for Kelly to come by tomorrow and take Bee to the Sights and Sounds Theatre. The play was *Joseph* and Bee knew the story well and had played a role in it at home in her community theatre. It would be so nice to meet this creative person who was the set designer's assistant.

They all held hands around the table and Grammpy said the blessing. He slipped back to his original Pennsylvania Dutch accent while praying. It was how he was used to praying from childhood and good to hear again.

The meal was delicious and very traditional. They had fried chicken, mashed potatoes and home made preserves. For dessert Grammpy had picked up a Shoo Fly pie from the bakery down the road. It was so sweet and so yummy. The bakery seemed out in the middle of nowhere and was frequented by many customers from all over America and Canada.

They helped with the dishes and enjoyed the interaction as they did them by hand. It was like camping, only better.

It had been a long day so Bee and Mom went to sleep early. Tomorrow would be an early day too. They didn't tell the elderly couple about the drama at home and at one point Grammpy asked what the bruises were on Bee's arms. He should have seen the rest of her body. She was becoming so black in spots. It was funny, but she didn't even feel she had to wear Amish clothing this time. She was reminded of how free Grammy and Grammpy where regarding others' life styles and how accepting they of them.

Then she remembered why they were here. It was to be safe and blend in. Grammy had Bee's clothes hanging in her wardrobe. The colour was Bee's favorite. Grammy had buttons sewn on the inside where they weren't noticeable. The Amish girls used straight pins to fasten their clothes and Grammy wanted Bee to have an easier time getting dressed, as she wasn't used to using those pins on her dresses and aprons.

Kelly would be here at 9 a.m. for a day out. Bee was looking forward to meeting her.

The ladies slept like babies and were refreshed in the morning, ready to help with breakfast. When they arrived downstairs, Grammpy already had everything done.

He took one look at Bee and smiled. He thought she looked just like her mom when she was her age. The plain, sky-blue dress and white apron made her eyes look more prominent and more beautiful than before. She had made a little bun in her long blonde hair and the little sheer white cap gave her a look of sophistication.

Grammy gave her a big hug and again told her it was *gut* to have her there.

Mom also wore her Amish outfit. It was a more subdued colour of a deep blue, almost black. Her apron was black and her cap was white. They both wore their sandals, which were just a little too modern to be authentic-looking. Bee had forgotten to remove her nail polish but said she would do it after breakfast.

Breakfast was delicious. Grammpy fried eggs and scrapple as well as some of that special homemade bread with Grammy's preserves.

They had to take turns brushing their teeth as there was only one bathroom, but it was inside.

Grammpy put a hot water tank in for the shower and a flush toilet, as well as a sink. It was so modern. Mom had to go outside to use the toilet when she lived there.

Even on her wedding day she didn't have an indoor toilet and shower or tub. The old galvanized tub still hung on the wall in the back entrance.

CHAPTER 26

Kelly

Bee heard someone loudly knock on the door down stairs from her room upstairs. *Wow, Kelly has a heavy hand,* she thought.

She rushed downstairs to meet the person who helped Grammy create her room. She stood frozen, her eyes scanning the room for the mysterious Kelly. Something didn't add up. *What was going on?*

Grammy came over and took Bee by the hand to meet Kelly.

"Kelly this is Bee and Bee this is Kelly."

Bee didn't know what to do! This was so awkward! Kelly seemed okay with it and told Bee how good she looked as an Amish single young lady. "Rumspringen years?" he asked her.

Everyone laughed except for Bee who wondered why she would look like she was in her Amish rebellious teen years.

Bee politely asked, "No, why?"

"Well you look so perfectly Amish except for your painted toe nails, yah?"

Bee had forgotten about them and started to laugh as she looked down at her plain outfit that ended up with her brightly painted hot pink toes.

Kelly told her he thought they looked *gut,* and was she ready?

As they walked out to Kelly's car, Bee was shocked when he accompanied her to the passenger side and opened the door for her to get in and then closed it for her.

It made her feel like this was a date or something.

Bee started to laugh out loud as she came to her senses and realized her confusion in thinking that Kelly was a girl.

Maybe the laugh covered her nervousness, but she couldn't stop herself.

"What are you laughing at?" he questioned with a totally puzzled look.

Bee told him she thought he was a girl and how shocked she was that he wasn't. She could hardly finish her sentence before she started up laughing again.

He said, "Should I go and change?"

They both laughed.

He wanted to take her to the theatre first and show her around as well as introduce her to the set designer. After all she had the ideas and put her stamp of approval on every piece that Kelly ordered for Bee's room.

Bee was in awe of how professionally the theatre was built. It was all done top-notch, to the highest quality.

Kelly took Bee's hand at one point to hurry her along and it almost seemed natural. He showed her where he played his part in the mechanical design, and told her how he was shunned because of his belief in a freer way of life. He loved designing the sets and going to the school of design, instead of farming.

His story of how he met Grammy and how she was so nice to him touched Bee. Grammy let him stay at the farm until he got on his feet after he was excommunicated from his church and his family and then shunned. She gave him a place to sleep in their home and fed him. Even more importantly, Grammy showed him the way to everlasting life. Bee listened quietly to the sad story.

Kelly saw her face and said. "Don't be so sad, I have more now than I ever had. All is *gut*."

Bee thought about how she would feel if she couldn't talk to her Dad or Mom or brother. They were interrupted when the set designer came by and they were introduced.

Grammy seemed to have the respect of so many people. Everyone talked about her helping, in various ways, even this designer.

They had perfect seats and enjoyed the energy of the show. Of course the sets were out of this world and the acting superb. Bee knew someone from her school who took acting in Lancaster and had acted in these plays. The story ended with the most marvelous message a person could hear.

"Everyone should go and see one of these plays," Bee said.

Afterward, they went to a fifties diner. It had the best burgers and great pies. They talked for hours and she got to know Kelly's past. He seemed like a nice young man and Bee had to ask him how old he was. He said he was going to be 20 years old this harvest season. October 1, to be exact.

He had three brothers and four sisters, and he was the eldest of them. Since he was the oldest, Kelly was to quit school after his eighth grade and take over some of the main work on the farm. His parents were old order Amish, but reformed to old Mennonite after they realized a new way of thinking and living.

"I can now speak with them and could live with them, but I was settled and *gut* on my own so I stayed that way. I have been on my own since I was 14 years old."

Bee couldn't imagine Josh on his own at 14 years of age, never mind herself at almost 17.

Kelly continued to tell Bee his story.

His parents changed their lives after Grammpy and Grammy shared their own philosophy of life and the Bible with them. They had never been allowed to read the Bible on their own, although their order believed it and the Bishop preached from it.

This was only a year ago.

He said it was good visiting his family, as many did not get that opportunity any more after they changed their life style.

As Bee and Kelly walked down the road after Kelly had parked the car, he took her hand again and they walked to a covered bridge. He explained about the history of the covered bridge and how it had been reconstructed to its original state just a couple of years before.

He felt it was important to keep one's heritage alive and not forget the good things about the past. He also reminded Bee that the tragic things of our past remind us of the adjustments we need to make in the future, so the same mistakes are not made over again.

Bee agreed. She was glad to listen, as she couldn't share all those things that had brought her to Lancaster. She could talk about her Dad and Josh, and her job and her Mega Church, Central Community Church. She later showed him how to access it and view it online at the town library. She loved her church, as did her family, and they were excited about the planned new building.

Talking about her Pa was too sad at this point. She was still emotionally unstable when she spoke of Pa and his disappearance.

There was a well-trodden path running along the creek and they walked slowly for about an hour. Then they sat down under a large tree with its wide branches relieving them from the hot afternoon sun.

Bee couldn't believe how easy it was to talk to Kelly. She felt a little awkward when their eyes happened to meet although she enjoyed gazing straight into his eyes. It seemed as though she could look deep into his soul. His eyes had so much compassion and spoke without words. At one point she braced her body with her hands at her side, next to his hand. She felt a flip in the pit of her stomach and moved immediately.

What was that? she thought.

She felt captivated. Her spirit was soaring, her heart was pounding and her mind was numb. She took a deep breath and forced her mind back to reality.

The time had worn on and she had to get back to Grammy's place. Like a gentleman, Kelly gave her his hand for getting up. It was so amusing to her that she would never have put being a gentleman on her list of attractive qualities, but somehow it sure seemed to catch her attention now. It was a natural response from Kelly as it backed up his feelings regarding respect for the opposite gender.

They walked back to the car in a quieter mood and Bee wondered what he as thinking about.

She told him that it was a lovely day and he said how good it was and that he enjoyed it too.

When he spoke, Kelly had such a believable tone to his voice. Bee silently wondered if she would be able to distinguish a lie if it should come from him?

She knew that wouldn't happen, as he would never lie to her.

They pulled into the farmyard where her mom and grandparents sat on the front porch relaxing.

Kelly got out and opened the door for her again.

They walked to the front porch and talked about the theatre, lunch and the rest of the day.

Grammy asked Kelvin to stay for dinner but he had made plans to eat with his family tonight since it was his day off. Bee was taken aback at the name Grammy called him and looked startled. Kelly explained he took on the name "Kelly" to suit his new American life style and then chuckled.

Everyone understood of course, but Bee was disappointed knowing he wouldn't join them.

The days went by quickly and Bee and Kelly couldn't stand being apart for even one day. After work he would pop by and they would sit on the porch for hours and talk. Mom and Grammpy would often join in the conversation as Grammy went to bed early. Bee was enjoying her stay here so much, although quite unaware of exactly what was happening to her.

Kelly was taking online courses and needed to work at his computer. He had finished his high school already and now he was taking university courses.

Bee spent hours at the library with Kelly. She helped him research and retrieve books for his studies. She was stared at in the library, as they didn't see too many Amish girls there. Most of them had to quit school after grade 8 or sooner, depending on their family needs.

CHAPTER 27

Grammy's News

One evening Kelly was dropping Bee off and Mom was on the porch. She looked upset. Kelly left and Bee stayed on the wide porch to have some evening conversation.

Mom told Bee to sit down because she had bad news to tell her. Bee thought it was about Dad or Josh, and gasped for air. Mom told her it was Grammy. She was seriously ill and could need some medical attention in the morning.

Bee was shocked!

Grammy was told that she needed some tests at the hospital and she didn't want to alarm them beforehand. She was weak and had pain in her chest when climbing the stairs.

Mom wanted Bee to know, as she would leave early with Grammpy to take her to the hospital for the day.

Bee was upset and wondered what the matter could be.

Bee blurted out, "Kelly can take you with his car."

She felt like he was family and knew he would not mind.

"I can call him, Mom."

Mom said they should be at the hospital at 9 a.m., and they would not have to leave as early in that case.

She ran to the outside phone to call Kelly. Of course, he would be glad to give Grammy and Mom a ride to the hospital. He would be there at 7 a.m.

Bee and Mom prepared for the morning breakfast as much as possible and then headed for bed.

Usually Bee went to sleep daydreaming about Kelly and their day, but tonight she was pre-occupied with concern over Grammy. She had to be all right. Pa believed all his life that if you prayed, God would answer. She believed if prayer had been tested for that long it must be true; she would find out for herself and do the same.

Before bed every night Bee took time to write in her close friend the diary. She couldn't wait to give all the details to Josh and Dad. They didn't even know that Grammy was not well.

CHAPTER 28

Our Ride Home

Dad and I had to get going as we had a good ride ahead of us, and that was after crossing the border back to Canada.

At the border, they didn't pay too much attention to us and we were off. It was a nice day and we would enjoy our ride along the river, but first we had to conquer Clifton Hill.

We loved taking our bikes up the hill and could not pass up the chance to race each other to the top. We had done this many times before, and I was very close to beating him. This might be the time. We were just a short distance out of our way and we were enjoying the freshness of the mist coming from the falls.

I had to concentrate on beating Dad.

We obeyed all the laws and were careful not to hurt anyone. I was half way up when a car stopped beside me and the passenger opened the door right in front of me. I slammed on my brakes and was fortunate not to go head first over my handlebars. The driver apologized and Dad was ahead of me. I got going as soon as I could and was catching up with Dad. This time I was going to win. I went biking often and my legs were gaining strength. Yes, I was ahead of him when I was cut off once more and Dad swerved around me.

Not again - he won once more!

When I pulled up to Dad he said, "That was quite some riding, Son, you won,"

"No I didn't Dad. You beat me."

"Well the way I look at it is you had more obstacles and even with them you were right behind me."

"Well, Dad, wait until next time and I really will win, fair and square as you say."

We crossed the street and faced the falls once more. We were on our way. It certainly was a scenic place to live. We biked down the hill again past the busiest falls intersection, filled with people from all nations. It was one of the most congested places I had ever experienced. You could hear the thunder of the falls and feel the moisture of its mist. Gratifyingly cooling on a hot day, like the one we were experiencing, especially after our race.

Near the walkway alongside the falls we could see the huge kiss. On top of the building sat the oversized Hershey Kiss, as it appeared to sweetly guard the border crossing. When I was much younger I would imagine the mound in front of me. I would chop away at it with an axe and gorge myself with as much chocolate as I could possibly eat. It was still an appealing fantasy.

We were so hot after our competitive exercise. I was enjoying being on this side of the road near the edge, where the powerful water rushing past created humidity that dampened our clothes and cooled us.

There stood the Buddha Temple on the other side of the road and the busses lined up trying to get into the parking area. It was a busy stop on the oriental bus tours.

The White Water Walk intrigued me and I recalled an outing with Pa down the 70-meter elevator, through the tunnel and then to the 305-meter boardwalk. The observation deck was so awesome and I looked right into the eye of the gigantic whirlpool! It is a Class 6 whirlpool as well as the longest stretch (3-5 meters) of standing waves in North America.

Pa had always seemed to be more intrigued by he 410-million-year-old rock formation towering beside us. We had so many memorable times together, Pa and I.

Next, we passed the Whirlpool Aero Car and Great Wolf Lodge. The Aero Car brought back weird feelings. One time Pa took me for a ride and we spotted a dead body tossed about in the rough water below. The body looked bloated and it made me feel creepy. It was the first time I had seen a dead body, even though it wasn't close. I was told the jet boats would pick the body up, although that gave me little comfort.

As for the Great Wolf Lodge, Bee worked there. She had her lifeguard certification and enjoyed her job while going to high school. She was conscientious and did her job with purpose. It was too bad she had to take time off on short notice. She hated to do that to her supervisor.

The helicopters were landing as more tourists boarded them to view the falls from above. It was something I had never done but someday hoped to.

The road took us past the golf course and we decided to stop at the Whirlpool Restaurant for a drink.

We felt like tourists, being joined by so many others enjoying the day with their families.

As we biked past the Niagara Glen I wondered what secrets its banks held. I know our riverbank did, so why couldn't there be more undiscovered secrets?

I was enjoying this trip as I let my mind wander, peddling and reminiscing, until I came to the Sir Adam Beck Generating Station. This is where it all started, or so we figured. The plans to blow up the hydro plant and the tunnels had caused our family a lot of pain. It would never look the same to me again.

"Where will we keep the bikes, so no one sees them?" I asked as I pulled up beside Dad.

"I thought we would put them in the hall where the slide is. It seems large enough, even if we had to use the slide for escape."

"Good idea, Dad."

"We must make sure not to leave tire tracks on the floor."

That was good thinking, I thought.

Dad said to make a mental list of all the supplies we should sneak into the house, wasting little time after arriving home. Totally preoccupied, I heard a bike bell behind me and the couple wanting to get by rang again. Of course I moved over, and they thanked me.

We decided we had better hurry, as someone we knew might come by and recognize us. That would wreck the whole plan. We took the back way through the park to our property. We put the bikes in the hiding spot and made sure the floor didn't show any dirt or movement.

We snuck to the storage shed and retrieved the small fridge, then the composting toilet. We put these in the same hall with the bikes until we could take them down.

Dad told me to get a couple of sleeping bags and pillows and whatever clothes I would need. He reminded me that we were going to rough it. I realized that, and it didn't bother me at all not having to brush my teeth or comb my hair. An occasional shower would be nice, though.

The hall was getting a little crammed so we moved the stuff into the study, and straight downstairs.

Dad suggested that we retrieve the food that was in our house. We weren't supposed to be there anyways. We did this and our little fridge was packed.

We took everything we could think of. I thought it felt a little like a huge sleepover party.

When we had all that in our hideaway we thought we should have a place to sleep.

"Omz and Pa had these 'beds to go.' Do you think they still have them?"

"They would be in the attic upstairs if they do."

We went to look and there they were, under a lot of stuff stored from another time. The beds had real mattresses instead of the blow-up ones, as Omz didn't like the air mattresses. She said they didn't give a good night's sleep, and when we visited she wanted us in our best form so we could have lots of fun.

"These are perfect, and we will be very comfortable, even more than I expected," Dad said looking pleased.

We realized it was a blessing to have the house and everything in it at our fingertips. Omz left everything in order and the house looked loved and cozy even when no one lived in it.

Down in our "living area" as we called it, we set up the fridge near the table and chairs. It was placed beside the old hutch, with a plastic pan for washing dishes on top. The soap was stored in the hutch and the tea towel hung on the fridge handle. It was starting to look like home.

We discovered an old washstand in the attic that would be highly useful in our daily routine. It even had room on it for the matching antique water pitcher and a place to hang a towel. The natural place for our beds seemed to be on the side near the polar bear rug. It just seemed like the logical spot for our cots. Dad brought down a small round table from Omz's storage, and put it between our beds. He even brought down a calendar from home, as he said we might need to keep track of the days.

The toilet—well, that was another thing—nowhere seemed good for that. Was there not a little spot anywhere? This place was so well designed and no bathroom. I could hardly believe that. We just left it in the middle of the room until we could come up with the perfect spot. We remembered the toilet paper, a pail for the composting materials, and a few plastic bottles and jugs for drinking water, toothpaste, soap and you name it.

It had been a long day; first the emotions of saying good-bye to Mom and Bee, then the bike ride, as well as moving all that stuff into our cozy hideaway.

We decided to retrieve some of the plans from the storage room and spend the rest of the evening studying them. Better yet, we thought we would bring the whole bunch of them into our quarters so they were handy. We both took a lantern, which made our walk through the tunnel well illuminated. In one section of the tunnel I noticed the smooth rock formation. It was in the area just about ten feet past the stairs from where we came.

"Hey, let's check this out!"

I felt the wall as Dad came back to join me.

CHAPTER 29

The You-Know-What

I was used to the routine by now. Push on the wall or stones. I went to work as Dad held his light and mine sat on the floor, for a good view.

"Here," I said. "This one will move."

It didn't push in, or move sideways. I pushed with my body, first to left then to the right. Nothing worked.

I pushed just beside the smooth area, and "Voila!" Success.

This section of wall backed up and slid to the side behind the smooth area. The smooth part of the formation was definitely meant to be a decoy wall. Dad and I got our second wind after this discovery.

"Do you think we will be gone long? I don't have my pouch with me." I said.

Dad said, "We should just stop, if we didn't want to go any further as we have nothing but time."

I thought to myself, *Like that is going to happen.*

It was an interesting room, as there was nothing in it. There was a hole in one corner and we wondered where it went.

Dad said he would get a pail of water and pour it down and we would find out if it went anywhere. He was back in no time with a pot of water from the spring.

"Down the hatch," I said as he poured.

It disappeared as quickly as he could pour it.

"Great drainage."

As Dad watched the water disappear he said, "This will be a wonderful private bathroom don't you think?"

I agreed and couldn't wait to get the "throne" set up. We would bring one of those little boxes to put our paper and whatever in. The drainage hole would be a great place to put the dishwater and other grey water.

"We should keep a lantern or flashlight in here, don't you think?"

"That would be good, and I will let you take care of that, Josh."

As we entered our living cave, bringing back only one lantern, we viewed the toilet in the middle of the room.

"I think it will look a lot better in the bathroom, don't you?" Dad chuckled. We took our flashlights, composting chemicals and paper, eliminating another trip.

The Johnny was set on the right side of the room with the chemicals in an old box beside it. It also held a pail and a plastic bag with toilet paper. On the left, we put the water bottles as well as a small shelf holding our toothbrushes, cup and toothpaste. Another plastic pan for washing hands and brushing our teeth was placed on a table identical to the one between our beds. They must have been used as a set in days gone by. The drainage hole was on the same side in the far corner and it was convenient for dumping our wash water. The bathroom cave looked cool too, even trendy, as it had that rustic yet modern look. We were all set and couldn't believe we now had a bathroom, of sorts.

We were off to get the drawings and plans again.

With both hands full, as well as carrying our flashlights, we made it back to the living quarters.

We had left the lamp on and it looked inviting as we entered. I once more daydreamed about the times Mark and I could stay down here. Dad had brought the Coleman heater and had started it before we left for the plans. The air was dryer and we could even take our jackets off. The person that built this place would have enjoyed the modern conveniences we added. It had a "log cabin in the woods" feel.

CHAPTER 30

The Paper Scrolls

Dad took out the scrolls of paper and said, "Let's quickly check through and put them in some kind of order."

There were some of the house and rooms and even the coach house and the demolished garden house. It was difficult to put them on a pile without studying them first.

There were other plans that looked like the lines or rifts in the rock and only foundations of the buildings. The mansion house, and even the coach house appeared on a few.

The demolished garden house, where Great-Opa and Great-Oma lived, was also sketched with adjoining lines. We noticed the line coming from the gazebo.

"I think what I thought was fault lines are tunnels, Dad. See, this one coming from where the gazebo is?

And here is the one we found under Pa's study. And see how it joins the gazebo tunnel and goes right to the edge of the rock wall of the gorge?"

Dad commented as he scratched his head, "Look, there appears to be a very small line where our bathroom is and the storage room is marked too."

"You haven't been to the gorge yet but I will show you tomorrow Dad. I don't know what we will do about that cougar though."

"We will also have to check out this line that seems to come back from there. It goes into the rock for quite a distance, and look it is marked with a large circle at the end of it."

"Do you think that is that huge cavern?" Dad mused with a furrowed brow.

"We didn't have a chance to check it out, since Mac got that concussion, not to mention the cougar," I added.

Dad noticed the lines going from the cemetery to the edge of the gorge, and one towards our room, but not quite. It didn't seem to touch. We wondered how you would access it from the cemetery.

It was difficult to get back to sorting and piling the papers into categories and it took all the self-control we could muster not to study the old scrolls.

We also had a pile of papers with writing. We did not take the time to read them but stacked them up. There were about ten of them.

Dad suggested we retrieve Pa's old translation book from the office the next day. It had German words translated to English. Dad used it when he was younger to assist in learning the German language.

"Well I have found nothing to give me any idea of why someone would want to endanger my family or why your Pa disappeared," Dad mumbled.

"We'll find something, Dad, don't you worry."

The papers with the wording looked aged and I wondered if they were from my Great-Opa's time. I pointed out the words on the side of some of them. We took those with the German script and put them in a separate pile.

Finishing up, we had groups of drawings with detailed sketches and piles of written papers. Some were recognizable and others we knew were yet to be discovered.

Still others showed where we would find more water springs including the one we had already discovered. It was interesting to see where the electric lines ran. We could see how intricate the job must have been to conceal them from sight.

CHAPTER 31

The Surprise Visitor

The door to the large box leading down to the tunnel and then down to the bathroom was open as well as the door to our storage room. It was easier than lifting the lid every time we needed the facilities or got supplies. Sound travelled well through the tunnel. We heard an unrecognizable noise and then a loud crash. We could feel a strong draft of air flowing past. Suddenly, our papers started to rustle and blow around. We were startled, and quickly but quietly went to see what had happened.

We closed the door behind us, and entered the tunnel below. The airflow calmed. With our flashlights on we quietly made our way into the storage room. We were shocked to find the outside door to the gazebo stairway tunnel open. Neither of us made a sound.

With a big swallow, Dad said, "You stay here and I will check it out. Get ready to retreat and close the door behind you," he whispered.

I nodded, and stayed close to the tunnel door ready to close it. Meanwhile our flashlights were off.

Dad, slowly and quietly, made his way to the other side of the room, towards the door. With his flashlight off he wanted to surprise whoever it was.

Our secret and finding out what happened to Pa was now in jeopardy.

Standing, with tension mounting in the blackened space, I was startled by a loud noise, and a moan from Dad. He tripped over something and fell. With the biggest *crack!* he hit the floor. I hoped he didn't crack his head open too!

My flashlight went on immediately. Frantically I scanned for Dad!

CHAPTER 32

Badly Beaten

I not only found one body on the floor, but two! Dad had tripped over someone.

Oh-no—it was Mark! He was under Dad, on the floor, out cold. Blood was pooling under his head. Dad was recovering from the unforeseen fall and, rubbing his head, looked down at the intruder.

Recognizing Mark, he jumped up.

"Josh come and help me get Mark to safety so we can check him over," he commanded.

Coming back to his keen sense of security he said, "Wait we should close the outer door first," forgetting that it closed quickly and automatically. There might be someone following him.

What a terrifying thought that was and I reminded Dad that it would be closed.

I held Mark's legs and Dad took his upper body, as we carefully took him to the other room. He was totally out and I started to get concerned about the bleeding. We had grabbed a towel before moving him and wrapped it around his head and it was soaking through.

We put him on one of the cots with a blanket under to soak up the blood. He looked terrible as his face was bruised, swollen, his nose looked broken, and he had a huge gash on the side of his head behind the ear.

Dad checked him over and yelled, "Get me the first aid kit." Putting on his gloves, he put his head close to Mark's mouth. He also watched his chest rise and fall. "Good, he is breathing, but must be in shock. Cover him up with a couple of the blankets and get used to watching his chest. If it stops, or changes let me know."

He checked the wound and concluded it was a flesh wound. Not a cracked skull as he suspected.

He applied pressure on the wound for at least 15 minutes. And checked it. The bleeding slowed but wasn't stopped. Sometimes I thought that his chest stopped rising but when I put my cheek to his mouth I could feel a faint breath.

Dad put something on the wound to clean it. Mark needed stitches so Dad got a needle and thread from our supply box and sterilized the needle. Mark was still out so it was a good time to stitch him up. Then we wrapped his head in gauze.

"Help me turn him on his side just in case he has internal bleeding, Son."

We gently rolled him slightly on his side and I put a pillow behind his back.

"Now we can only wait and see," Dad spoke with a troubled look.

"Do you think he should go to the hospital?" I replied.

"I've been thinking the same thing myself, Son."

"We closed all the doors didn't we? Now, Mac is the only one that knows how to get in here. Right? Except for Mom and Bee?" Dad demanded.

"Do you think someone is trying to get in here, or followed Mark, Dad?"

"I sure hope not."

We kept the heater near Mark to keep him warm. Dad did all he could for now. He bowed his head and audibly prayed for God to intervene to improve Mark's condition and bring him back to complete health.

I prayed along with Dad in my usual silent fashion. Dad went to make us something to eat. My job was staying at Mark's side every second.

We wouldn't be able to relax, even a little, until he came to. It seemed like an eternity, but the clock said it was four hours later when Mark started to moan.

My heart jumped for joy. My friend was going to make it. We tried talking to him to bring him around. After many times of falling back into his quiet dreams he tried opening his eyes.

"Mark, Mark, open your eyes!"

He tried hard, but one was totally swollen shut, and the other barely opened because of his injuries.

"Can you talk?" I asked.

He nodded ever so slightly.

"First, what happened?"

He said, "Vinnie."

"Who?" Dad prodded with as gentle a nudge as he could.

"Is that the guy you wanted a police check on, Josh?"

Mark continued, "He wanted me to tell him where you were going, and to tell your secret. I told him I didn't know where, and didn't know what he was talking about."

"He said he would beat it out of me, even if it meant killing me. He pulled the large door down and was beating me in the garage when Mom came home, so he left me until later. He didn't want her to come looking for him and find me. I passed out on the floor. He had punched me in the ribs, face and head before he hit me with something hard. I came to when he was inside the house. I heard him telling Mom about not parking in the garage, as he needed the car later."

"I left through the back door of the garage and just wanted to run away. All I could think was that I would be safe here, in your hideaway, and he would not find me. I figured they would all think that I ran away, and wouldn't know why."

"Boy Mark, I'm glad you're safe and made it this far. You must stay here with us, until this is all over, you know.

He tried to look at me and said, "That's okay."

"Your mother is going to be worried about you, but we cannot tell her where you are."

Saying this, Dad checked Mark's ribs one more time and then wrapped them in case they were cracked. Blood from his head wound was soaking through the gauze so we changed it again.

Carefully feeling his nose, as it was still swollen and very tender, Dad told Mark when the swelling went down a bit he would have to set his nose and it would be as good as new.

"Josh, you stay here with Mark and I will get us another mattress and sleeping bag. It will give me a chance to see if someone is snooping around up there. No matter what, do not come after me."

I agreed. He left through the study tunnel, closing the door behind him.

Mark dozed off again. As I was trying to find the face I knew, I wondered how a person could look so different. He was unrecognizable. He had been such a good friend to me and I always knew that I could put my life in his hands and now he had proved it. It must have been terrible to endure that almost deadly beating.

I was so grateful that Vinnie had not accomplished his goal and killed Mark.

Dad snuck up to the attic to get another cot, mattress, sleeping bag, blanket and pillow. He would have to make two trips. On the way, he took some time to scan the area to check and see if anyone was around. Everything looked clear and he continued his way back down. He thought with all the planning it took to build the passageways they should have made one right from the top to bottom of this house. For all he knew there could be one and they had not yet found it.

When he was back with the bed and other gear he said we should give Mark something light to eat.

I went and got a can of soup from the cupboard and a cup of milk from our little fridge.

"Mark, it's too bad we have no straws," I apologized. "Your mouth must be sore."

He tried to sit up, but didn't have the energy. We put a couple of pillows behind him, to prop him up. Dad would give him little sips with a tablespoon, after the soup was warmed.

"Not too hot, Josh, I don't think he can take it."

"Okay," I replied.

Dad said everything looked quiet on top and we should settle in for the night. We had questioned Mark about closing the loose boards on the gazebo. He remembered struggling with them and was positive he had. He always carried a flashlight in his pocket and had used it to find the tape marking the secret door.

"You did well Mark."

Dad would check on Mark every hour and if I woke I was to do the same. It reminded me of the dreadful night with Mac's concussion.

Mark was fine through the night and had a much clearer mind the next morning. We had our breakfast and decided we would have to stay close for Mark's sake. Maybe when he was a little better we could leave him for the day to investigate the tunnels.

Dad studied some more plans while I cleaned the dishes and dumped the water down our cave plumbing system. I told Mark of our modern toilet and I thought I almost saw a smile break through his distorted camouflage-coloured face.

Settled in side by side we studied the lines once more. It certainly piqued our curiosity again when we stared at the line from the family cemetery. It angled to what looked like this room.

"How could this be Dad?" I said. "We played at that cemetery and never saw a thing."

"Well, Son we have been in and out of this house for years and didn't know about the tunnel from the study. And look at the line to the coach house. That really gets me, Josh."

CHAPTER 33

The Caretaker Spy

We decided to get working on the written papers. Dad found one called, *War Spy Orders,* and started a new pile. He read how the orders were to destroy the power supply by blowing it up with explosives. It was addressed to the "Caretaker."

"Was that Opa, Dad? Wasn't he a caretaker here?"

He said that he hoped not and we kept on reading. It said there would be more orders detailing a date in the future.

We went on to read another.

The next one talked about the Caretaker leaving and going back to his homeland. He was to abort the mission and destroy everything.

We found the date and it came after the first document and so we put it in order.

The next written page sounded like a reprimand, as it again specified for the Caretaker to destroy everything so nothing was left for evidence. It warned that there would be grave consequences if orders were not followed. There was word of tickets being sent, and the caretaker and his family would be accompanied back by an undercover agent. It was placed in between the last two letters.

"Hey it couldn't have been my Great-Opa. He didn't go back to Germany, right? He stayed here until he and Great-Oma died."

"That's right," Dad replied as he rifled through more papers.

The next one mentioned some gold that was sent to support,

"The Cause", and to buy supplies and explosives. It also mentioned the men who were sent, from the Fatherland, to do the labour.

The men would arrive two at a time and be kept blind folded once they arrived at the estate and be taken down into the shaft. They were to start at the natural shaft and work their way to directions they were given. They were to be hidden and not seen the whole time they were here. They were to be paid and fed well and, as the papers revealed, they should be quietly done away with after the work was done. The Caretaker could have the money he had paid them. They were handsomely paid to keep their spirits and work at a high level while alive in the tunnels.

"Can you believe that!" blurted out of my mouth, in uncontrolled amazement.

We discussed the fact that it had to be someone who could hide men and bring in supplies without anyone being suspicious. Maybe the German couple, that built the mansion or the garden keeper who lived there before Great-Opa.

We were making headway in finding the order of things. We still had no information that led to the disappearance of my pa.

We found a document that affirmed and congratulated the job well done, and instructions to silence the labourers. They were to be sent to a cave that was to collapse and kill them. If not killed outright, they could starve to death.

"How cruel. Whoever it was had to have been a monster!" I shouted in outrage.

"That is for sure," came a voice from behind, startling us.

It was Mark and he was sounding a little stronger.

"Where did you get this stuff from?"

"It was in the storage room," I told him.

We both looked back at him as he was trying to get up. He said he needed the bathroom and had we thought about that part of life for our hideaway?

"Don't you remember that I told you we have a toilet if you needed one?"

"No I guess I don't." Dad and I helped him up and he could stand

and slowly walk. Dad went first with the light and Mark followed him, with me by his side holding him tightly by the arm. The steep steps were the hardest.

"Where are we going?"

He turned the bend and entered our bathroom, his swollen achy jaw dropped for just a second, and he said, "Ahh, awethome," with tight lips and swollen tongue.

We gave him privacy and waited outside the room after lighting the lantern. I remembered what tipped us off to someone being down here and said," Do you remember the draft we felt before we went to check out the storage room?"

"It's a good thing you reminded me. We should find out where the air current gets through." We realized there must be a place the air was flowing through our living area.

We took Mark back to bed for a good night's sleep after using our totally unique toilet chamber. Our bodies also needed the rest and it was going to feel awesome to hit our mattresses. Our minds were worn out from trying to read between the lines and connect all the facts.

Our discussion in bed consisted of making a list of the things we needed to do. Dad wrote them down. They were: find the cause of the draft we felt, find the tunnel from the graveyard, find the tunnel to the coach house and find the large cavern as well as the money, if there was any. Of course our number one purpose would be to find out who was trying to hurt our family and what happened to Pa.

"Mark, we don't want you to get up on your own, so let us know if you need anything," Dad insisted.

He agreed, "I will."

Dad reminded him that he would wake him many times this night, just as a precaution.

Mark replied, "It will be just like when I was in the hospital with appendicitis."

"I hope you are not that sick!" I insisted.

He thought he was in much better shape, except for the bruising.

CHAPTER 34

Desperation

Mark's mom was beyond being in control. The police questioned her at two o'clock in the morning, after she had hounded them with four separate phone calls in an effort to get them to find her son. She had no idea to where and why Mark had disappeared. The police said they found some blood stains in the garage and questioned her about them. She had no idea what they were talking about. Vinnie was also questioned with great scrutiny but of course had an alibi. He told the police he had a buddy helping him with the lawn mower and the guy cut himself and it bled a lot. The police surmised Mark was probably out with a friend dismissing Angelica's insistence that her son would not do such a thing without her permission.

Her stomach ached and her mind was going in circles, thinking horrifying thoughts and then praying for Mark's safety. What should she do? She ran over to Josh's place but there was no one home. She knew that he would know something.

Vinnie seemed to be very preoccupied. He couldn't figure out what happened to Mark either, but needed to stop him before he told anyone about his beating and the threats. He needed to work fast as things had spun out of control.

He had worked too hard to locate his missing ancestor and perhaps find the money. Killing the elderly lady would definitely send him to prison. All he could think of was to find the gold and escape.

The guy he hired to assist him had just cost him money and had bungled the job he had assigned him to. He couldn't even kill the girl, and now they didn't have access to her. The police were on his tail. He would have to get rid of his accomplice after they targeted their next victim.

What would he do with that nice new truck? He could have it painted and make a few changes to it. His anger exploded from within as he thought about how many mistakes were made. He had to act fast, if he would achieve his goal. Nothing would stand in his way.

Angelica tried to find comfort in Vinnie, as her last living relative, through this most terrible time in her life. Vinnie seemed to show hate and anger towards her every minute he was around. He was out for most of the day and it left her to her own thoughts of turmoil and frustration.

She heard Vinnie yell on the phone in anger and say they would have to, "...finish the job."

She was scared and had nowhere to turn. The police didn't seem to think that she knew her son, except for Barry of course. He would keep his ears and eyes peeled for her and checked in daily to see if she had any news from Mark.

Mac also came by and said she would be back every day. One day she didn't show up and Angelica missed her compassionate conversation. Angelica didn't know which day it was, as the days were running into each other and causing a blur in her mind and memory.

How could this happen? She was so alone and lost. There were no more tears left to cry and she felt numb as she went about her daily chores. She didn't care if the laundry got done or if she ate a meal. Nothing mattered anymore. She needed to get her son back and now feared something terrible had happened to him. He would never put her through this much pain if he had a choice.

CHAPTER 35

The Cemetery

After breakfast Mark was feeling much better than the night before, except for his bruising, and swelling of course.

We told him I would be investigating the graveyard and Dad would stay here and study some more papers. He was glad to be safe, and rested for most of the day. It was good for his body to take the time to heal.

I went up to the study, and then quietly snuck back into the kitchen. From the windows, I could have a clear view to the graveyard in the distance and the tall trees above it. It was still very early and the sun was not fully up yet. Carefully scanning the area to see if anyone was snooping, I noticed how peaceful it looked. The uncut grasses swayed gently under the dark tree canopy. The tall covering seemed to be a barrier from the rising sun, darkening all that was beneath. The stacked stonewall separating the property from the road could barely be seen.

Exiting the mansion through the back kitchen doors, I once more stepped onto the grand porch. Passing the aged wicker rocker, my heart yearned to sit in it once more with Pa beside me. My mind was wandering and I needed to concentrate. Shaking off all those sentimental thoughts, I made my way along the ridge of the gorge to the graveyard.

The first thing I would do was take time to fix that spout. I would need my flashlight so early in the morning, but didn't want to be seen. For this reason I decided to sit behind a bush out of sight and enjoy the morning air.

I let my mind wander where it wanted to and imagined Bee in her Amish dress. She would hate every minute of it, but she would be the best-looking Amish girl there, that's for sure!

Then I thought of the men that died unknowing. They worked so hard for years, unseen and never saw their reward. How terrible for their families not to know their demise. I would feel totally lost without my dad, and so would the rest of the family. My thoughts were fixed once again on my purpose.

It was a beautiful morning and the dewy grass fed my sense of smell, as the moist trees provided that damp cool feeling adding to my above ground experience of this day.

Telling myself to concentrate, I neared the family plot and looked over the edge of the gorge, wondering where the tunnel opened to the gorge wall below. I directed my attention back to the first task at hand. It was of course, to fix that faucet.

Then I would do a search for the tunnel from this cemetery to the gorge or towards our secret room. That was how the lines looked on the sketch we looked at. I really didn't know where to start.

It was such a peaceful spot and I could picture the gardener's cottage right here. The door would have been facing the main house. I was told it had two little porches, one on the gorge side and one on the side facing the mansion. The gorge side porch would have made a nice place to sit, especially on moonlight summer evenings after the hard days of work.

The granite was so clean, having been washed by rain and bleached by the sun. I stepped in front of the main stone, looking closely at the flowers in the basket and that crooked tap.

It ran continuously, which made me wonder if it must be fed by a spring instead of a circulating pump, like I first imagined. I went to work fixing it first. The pressure needed on the tap didn't seem too great. It turned and my work was done. It flowed and rippled over in a small cascade of soothing babble. Why had it not been fixed before?

This was easy. At its feet lay a companion granite basin, which continuously maintained just enough water. It was designed so beautifully, and the nice thing was, it needed little maintenance. My job was done, and it didn't take long at all.

My eyes caught sight of Omz's grave; it was closest to the gorge and looked newer than the other two. Hers had a picture on it. It brought back such fond memories of her fair, soft hair, the fragrance of her perfume, aromas of food, loving touches and just that energetic atmosphere that accompanied her.

Then I went to look at my Great-Oma's grave. It was next to my Great-Opa's. Hers was plain but had a smaller basket of flowers similar to my Great-Opa's. It also sat on a beautiful large piece of granite. I put my hand under the carved greenery to see if it too had a hollowed pocket, like that of Great-Opa's. Carefully with my one hand, I explored. There was a loose piece of stone inside, and yet it was attached. This was odd. I stood on the granite right in front of her stone and bent low to see inside the cavity. I shone my flashlight, holding it close to the hollow, so no one else could see too much light if they happened by.

I tried to pry it loose. Suddenly the granite slab under me gave way and tilted downward away from the monument. I slid down as before, but this time into a fast-moving water stream.

I couldn't grab onto anything, and twisted and twirled and dropped as the water forced me helplessly and dramatically downward. I remembered the drawing of the tunnel that showed it going right out to the edge of the gorge. I hoped that was not where I was headed. Would I be able to stop myself? The drop of the water was extreme as it forced me to surrender. The water stream moved so rapidly and I couldn't see anything, except a small light in the distance. The worn sides and bottom gave me little to hang on to.

I tried to put my legs out to the sides. My hands stretched out to bridge the rock walls and stop myself. It took everything I had to stop my momentum. There was nothing left in me but it worked. *What now?* The force of the water was trying to pry me loose, but I braced myself as hard as I could. How long could I resist its power?

Scaling downward, against the wall in a snow angel fashion I let the water push me down as I resisted its pressure. It was a grueling task but there was no other way.

I had to let the water take me, and to where I didn't know. Trying to control my fate, I stiffened my body. I was now only moving in a slightly downward direction, as it was leveling off. The force of the water was gaining power. It was all I could do to barely hang on. My muscles ached, and I could feel my arms and legs shake. The light was getting closer. Maybe this was why the water was gaining such force.

It would take me with it, right over the gorge.

Now I was earnestly praying. *Help me, Lord!* Pa prayed and he believed his prayers were heard, and answered. Now I was in a position to do the same.

Nearing the opening, I could see daylight ahead of me. How far was it and what should I do?

Suddenly, I saw a rope hanging on the inside of the small tunnel. Could I grab it in time? *Should I let go?* I was scared to let go of those walls. Yes, I would try! God gave me a way out, and I would take it. I believed that with my whole being.

I let go with my hands, but kept my feet tight against the walls and reached. My feet weren't holding. Lunging upward, as hard as I could, I caught the rope in my hands. My heart was beating so hard I thought it would come right out of my chest as both my numb hands clenched the rope tightly.

I noticed a couple of other things as I had time to collect my thoughts. The light had enabled me to see. I wouldn't have seen the rope without it!

Hanging on with my hands twisted in the rope, I tried to look around and get my bearings. To my right was a dark hole that looked like some kind of ledge. It was about two feet up. At this point I couldn't see what was above the ledge, but if it was large enough I could rest my body on it. If I could manage the climb up out of the water, I would gather my strength to go on.

My arms were like rubber and I couldn't feel my hands. They were so tightly wrapped in the rope by now that I couldn't even move them. Taking a deep breath, I thought of Pa and how he said there were two ways out of a place. It gave me new strength, enough to untangle my hands and methodically climb the rope, placing one hand after the other.

Maybe this would be another way out instead of over the edge of the gorge. It definitely would be an answer to my prayer. Just one more burst of energy to lift my weight up to the top of the ledge. I willed my hands to climb, as I couldn't feel them. One movement at a time, my body was raised to the height of the stone ridge. Arriving on the hard floor, I lay there. I had no alternative but to do so. My head turned and peered into the darkness. I looked back at the light and the water stream.

I thanked God for the light, even though it was one of the scariest moments in my life. The rope I was still holding onto tightly seemed to go directly into the black hole. I gently tugged on it. It must be fastened somewhere in that dark hollow. I needed my flashlight to see where it led.

My flashlight, where is it?

CHAPTER 36

Blinded by Darkness

I had it in my hand when I dropped into the water, and must have lost it. I would have to depend on the rope to lead me into the darkness. I was frightened but knew there were no other alternatives. Would the rope lead me to a drop off, or would I have to jump a crevice in the rock while hanging on? How would I even see it? This must be what blind people feel like, nothing but blackness.

Every step was carefully executed, as one foot at a time was shuffled to move forward.

Oh, I wished I had my flashlight. Encouraging myself, the words, "I can do this," boldly and loudly, sounded out of my mouth. I would make it.

It seemed to take forever as I kept on putting tension on that rope and pulling myself forward. At one point, there was something I stumbled over. It seemed heavy and didn't move. Not being able to see, I just kept going.

Finally, the end of the rope! I felt two large bolts. Without dropping the rope, my only security, I let one hand explore. It felt like a wide, rough plank. Quickly the rope was blindly wrapped around my ankle, I just needed to know where it was. Continuing, I felt many boards all running in the same direction. All seemed to have nails holding them in place.

I pounded on the wood. Who would hear me, way down here?

No one!

Out of frustration I kicked the door repeatedly. Keeping my head was difficult and took all I had left in me. Realizing I might need two hands and two feet, I secured the rope around my waist. I thought of some of the small tool-like objects I had in my pouch. Digging through it in the dark, I couldn't make out the piece that I wanted. I was so frustrated.

Suddenly, I heard a loud noise. It sounded like someone had kicked the wood from the other side. I kicked back hoping that whoever it was, was friendly. I had no options but this one, so I kicked again. Whoever it was replied. I heard someone working with a hammer and then pulling nails. Standing in the darkness I could hardly wait to be released from the darkness and my isolation.

The light streamed into the darkness, as one board was pulled free. I quickly but reluctantly stuck my head through the plank to find . . . Dad!

"Dad its you!"

"Josh, are you alright?" called Dad.

"I am now," I replied.

He only needed to remove two wide planks and I could squeeze through.

The planks were behind one of the animal skins and in front stood the huge old kitchen cupboard.

"Did you find another passage way?" asked Dad.

"Not one that I ever want to take again."

We assumed after my description of the water passage that it didn't meet up with this one because of its dangerous drop at the end. It must have a purpose, or why build it?

CHAPTER 37

Mark's Nose

Getting out of my wet clothing I hung it on chairs to dry out. Dad wondered if we should nail the passage shut but I suggested we look at it with some flashlights later. He just hung the furs back and returned the cabinet to its place, after I asked him not to do that.

Now that my life was no longer in danger, my curiosity piqued. What caused me to stumble in there? After telling them of my grueling experience, I remembered my flashlight.

"I also dropped my flashlight in the water."

"What!" Mark got excited, as he replied, "It could have been your flashlight. I saw a light as I was pouring water down the hole. The light was there, and then, before I knew it, it was gone. If that is the case, the water runs under our bathroom and over the gorge. Ooh! We thought it was clean water from the springs that flowed out of the rocks and over the gorge."

We chuckled at our discovery. I had been gone for hours and noticed Mark's face and nose looked much better as far as the swelling went. Dad said he was glad I was back because he had to reset Mark's broken nose.

Mark looked a little worried, but said, "I guess if you can go through what you did today, I can do this." He lay down and Dad went over and put his hands on either side of his nose. One, two, three, and there was a crack.

We heard a small, "AHHH!" but it was not as bad as I first thought it would be for him.

"You are a real trooper, Mark. It will heal quicker now and feel better too. Just try not to bump it okay?"

Mark would have to take it easy for a few more days, but he was on the road to recovery. His face was bruised and puffy, and his eye still closed. His ribs felt good and we assumed they were not broken.

We had a small meal and Dad and I talked about what we would do next.

CHAPTER 38

Planning for Tomorrow

Dad had studied a drawing of a huge cavern that was somewhere down below. He wanted to know what it contained.

I reminded him of the cougar, so he gave us some tips if we should encounter the beast. We would take some gunpowder with us since it would be fearful of the fire. Dad told me not to run as it might spark the animal's hunting instinct. We would try to make ourselves look large while facing it. He said to keep our voices as low-pitched as possible and at the same time, throw rocks or anything else to scare it. Boy, I hoped I could remember all this stuff.

We gathered our supplies and put them into two backpacks. We checked our batteries and packed a snack.

We would leave first thing the next morning, if Mark remained well enough to stay alone.

Dad told him if we were gone for longer than he thought we should be, he could go to Barry and he would protect him. Mark could not tell Barry about our secret place, as then Bee and Mom would be in danger. He understood and promised to do as we said. He also said he would stay put until we got back in what we thought would be a few hours.

We spent the rest of our time studying the sketches and reading some of the letters. It was a relaxed time as we were packed for the next day and had no real bedtime. When we got tired we went to bed.

CHAPTER 39

Adventure for Mark

His face in new green, blue and yellow colours, Mark looked quite strong the next morning. We had breakfast and we noticed Mark's new energy had returned.

We decided to take it slow so he could join the expedition for the day. It would be easier to have him with us than wonder how he was doing by himself. He could carry the lantern for us.

It was Mark's first time exploring down below as well as Dad's. This would be fun. We took the steps from the supply room and went down, down and down, winding and turning until we hit the open cavern.

The one where the cougar lives? We crossed to the other side being as quiet as possible. Crossing the wet area, we were careful not to slip. We had made it to the tunnel with two directions.

One way went to the gorge and the other—well—we were going to find out. I showed Dad the place where Mac and I hid out for the night.

Dad signaled for us to stop and he took a little bit of gun powder and put a line of it all the way back to the cavern. He said we could light it if we ran into the cougar. He said to look for cougar tracks too.

We moved on into the unexplored cave. It was dark and we certainly needed our lantern and flashlights. The tunnel seemed to be mostly on one level but wound around back and forth a lot.

"Keep your eyes open for any different markings or stones or anything else," Dad cautioned.

It seemed like it took forever to find anything different. Dad reminded us that we had all day.

This was exciting and my heart was pounding at the thoughts of what we would find.

CHAPTER 40

The Large Cavern

The sound of our footsteps changed and there seemed to be an echo.

In a couple of steps our eyes beheld the most awesome sight.

It was that gigantic, huge cavern we saw on the plan.

"Can we explore it?"

"Boys, I want us to stay together, do you understand?"

In unison, we both said, "Yes sir."

We lit the extra lantern and held both of them high to look around.

"It is gigantic, enormous, *gi-normous*!" I couldn't find words to describe it so I made one up.

There were no stalactites, nor stalagmites, like there are in some caves I had seen in books. It was a vast open cave. It was the likes of one the pirates would have lived in and used to hide their treasures.

Mark started to laugh, "Wahoo, can you believe this?"

We couldn't wait to explore it.

Dad asked for my compass and we decided to go one way all round, first keeping track of our direction.

We also decided to keep one lantern right there, where the cavern met the tunnel. The light would shine for quite a while and give a sense of how far we had gone. It had enough fuel to last us a few hours. We had no idea what we would find.

Dad had the compass, paper and pencil. I had the lantern and Mark a flashlight. Dad was wearing the headband-light that I had retrieved from my room for just this purpose.

We started out with the wall on our left and carefully made our way along the perimeter of the cave following it.

It seemed to have no signs of life, not even a rag or twig or anything. We spoke quietly as if someone would hear but our whispers echoed.

We spotted something.

There was another dark tunnel.

Dad thought we should go around the perimeter first and come back, so we kept on going. I hoped it wasn't a mistake. My curiosity was piqued, as I wondered where it led.

CHAPTER 41

The Underground Pool

We could hear water dripping in the distance. As we neared, our lights were reflected in an underground lake. It looked to be about the size of four quite large swimming pools. We stopped, being very careful not to slip. We took a minute to study the lake's surroundings. Everything looked the same, just stone and more stone, except for the lake, of course.

"Do you think the water is good to drink?" I asked, kneeling on the rock floor.

It looked deep and felt cold. It didn't seem to move or flow, so we didn't know how good it was, although there was no foul odour.

We decided to keep going around its perimeter. There seemed to be a ledge on the far side of the small lake between the rock wall and the water. It looked like it was wide enough for us to get around the lake.

"Dad we haven't checked out the whole perimeter if we don't check out this part!"

He agreed and we carefully moved forward. Where the ridge narrowed, our lights fell onto an opening in the rock. It ran low to the ground and parallel with it. Near the bottom of the rock wall, quite close to the water, was a horizontal cleft in the rock. It seemed about seven feet long and approximately two feet high.

We decided to have a look, and knelt with our heads near the ground. We shone our light in as we saw another space on the other side.

"Can we go?" said Mark

Dad and I chuckled at Mark who was so enthusiastically on board.

"This is not the perimeter but, let's do it," Dad conceded.

He had the light on his head so he went first being able to see clearly. Taking his backpack off, he had to lie on his back and shuffle his way to the other side. Once there he scanned the area and waved for us to come through. I took my pack off too and pushed it through as far as I could.

Mark went headfirst and with a low body crawl, got through. I passed my lantern to them and went the same way as Dad, pulling my waist pouch to the front and on top of my body. I didn't want to crush its precious contents.

CHAPTER 42

Signs of Life

We stood and stretched as we repositioned our backpacks and took note of our supplies to make sure they were still in good order.

With great anticipation, we used our lights to scan the room. This cave was different. Around the corner of huge jutting bolder we found signs of life. You couldn't see this when peering in from the outside as its contents were completely hidden from view. There was a cot, sleeping bag, cans of food and a place where a fire had burned.

The ashes were cold.

"Wow, who was down here?" I uttered in awe.

Mark started to look around and pick up stuff to see if he could find answers. He checked the sleeping bag to see if something was in it, but nothing. Dad checked to see if there was another way out.

It was a nice size cave. Our lights made it appear somewhat cozy. I noticed the cans were stacked neatly and the used ones also, in another area. The sleeping bag and pillow were straightened out crisply—that was before Mark messed them up in his search. There was a long wooden stick that looked like it was used to poke the fire. A pail stood close by, filled with water.

"I don't get it Dad. Who lives here and where are they now?"

Dad was preoccupied with a box and its contents. He didn't even hear me.

"Dad, what did you find?"

As I shone the light towards him, I realized he was as pale as a ghost.

"Are you alright?" I questioned.

He almost fell to the ground, catching himself just enough to break the fall. We ran over to him.

"Are you alright?" Mark cried out not caring about the loudness of his voice.

I held his shoulders and as I sat on the floor beside him. "Tell me Dad, what is the matter?"

Mark's eyes searched in the box where Dad had been.

"Is this what upset you?"

He lifted an old Bible. "Isn't this your Pa's, Josh?"

"Yes!"

Dad's head cleared a little, and he reached out for it. He paged through it carefully, as though it would bring Pa back to him.

"Do you think Pa lives down here? Or could someone have stolen it?"

"I don't know, let me think for a minute and try to figure this out."

We knew Dad needed some space right now so we left him there to collect his thoughts. The two of us looked around. In one corner the darkness seemed denser than everywhere else. Our lights revealed a passageway.

"Dad, come here. It's another tunnel!"

I ran over to him.

"Maybe if Pa is down here, we can find him, Dad!"

He slowly got up, and with great care put the Bible in his sack.

His energy was coming back as my words resounded over and over in his head, "We can find him."

Dad went first and we followed close behind.

It was a walkable tunnel, although not wide. It was comfortable for the width of one at a time, and it suited us just fine.

"Here look at this!" Dad shouted.

We couldn't see ahead of him, so we replied, "What? We can't see."

"I'll move ahead and you move up," he replied. It was a hollow in the wall, about three feet deep and high and five feet wide. Dad crouched and squeezed into it. We did the same. In one corner near the back wall lay a lantern and a box.

"Wow, what's in that?" shouted Mark.

CHAPTER 43

The Old Chest

"Let's see," he said as he neared the box. It looked ancient, just like a treasure chest, with old tarnished brass corners and brass straps across it. The oversized lock was strong and heavy. We wondered if we could break it. Quickly I rummaged through my bag.

"Here is my screwdriver, will it help?"

Dad started to work at the bolts on the chest, which had an old worn, leather wrap on it. He couldn't loosen the bolts. We tried to lift it and see if we could shake it. It was heavy but manageable. It shook like there were coins inside.

Dad suggested we take it with us and try to open it back in our retreat.

"Can we just go to the end of this tunnel, Dad?"

"Yes, I think we should, and come back for this after we get to the end."

We backed up and stood straight stretching our backs. We didn't realize how tense our bodies had become, in all the excitement.

Our lights shone forward, leading us further and further into the darkness. Everything looked the same, as huge shadows played on the irregular rock formations.

Dad stopped as he heard something, and whispered, "Shhhh."

We listened but heard nothing.

Then we heard it.

We all heard something.

It was an odd sound.

Like something was scratching.

Our bodies tensed.

Moving forward, I stepped on Mark's heel, and gave him an apologetic whisper.

"Sorry."

The scratching sound came closer and closer, until we thought we were on top of it. I mean, literally on top of it. It was a rock floor but we heard scratching! There was someone or something below us.

Dad suggested we go back and take the chest, look at our plans of this area and see where the tunnel led. We nodded, and carefully turned back. It took quite some time to carry the chest back along the narrow tunnel, which was only wide enough for one person, as well as push it through the low crevasse in the rock. We picked up the lantern on the way back through the main tunnel going up. The small trunk was sure heavy enough, as we changed hands many times and stopped often to rest.

When we arrived, our intrigue got the better of us. We took the tools that would be useful for the job and locked the doors. We were safe except from whoever lived down there.

CHAPTER 44

The Chest is Opened

We all stood as if frozen around the old chest. Although our minds went hundred miles an hour, now was the time to act. Dad took a chisel and started to work on an old bolt. It was certainly well constructed. One of the nails, or should I say bolts, finally gave way and popped off. They looked like they were hand-forged and hammered into place. We figured if we could get the other one off we would be able to lift the lid. We were so tense and highly excited.

Mark started to jump and Dad had to tell him, "Stop!" as he was still too fragile for that kind of jolting to his body.

We could hardly contain our enthusiasm.

"There we go," Dad sounded, almost boasting.

He put the pliers under the lid and started to lift it. I took the other side and did the same. It suddenly gave way to our persistence and the other bolt went flying. We all jumped, as the unexpected movement startled us. "Wow!" said Mark.

"Look at that," I answered.

"What do we have here?" Dad laughed.

It was a chest full of old pre-World War 2 coins. They were mostly German and some were Russian, and then we found some French ones.

"Are these worth a lot of money?" I asked.

Dad thought they would be and Mark and I started to make piles as we counted them. Of course, that wasn't so quickly done.

"Are these gold?" I asked.

"They sure look like they are," Dad replied.

Dad went to his backpack and spoke sadly, "I would give up all the gold, just to find out what happened to Pa."

As Dad took out Pa's Bible and looked for some kind of clue, he deliberated, "A man just doesn't disappear in thin air!"

"Yes, he does, Dad, just look at the two of us and Mark."

Dad looked at me with a puzzled look and then, as if the light went on, replied, " Yes, and he might be here somewhere! He might have had to hide like we did!"

I went back to counting.

Mark lay down to rest, with a couple of coins still clutched in his hand. It was quite a strenuous and emotional day for him. After some time, we realized it was pointless to sort the coins, as we would have to put them back in their chest to hide them again. Next time we would bring some plastic bags to do the job.

"Back to studying the tunnels again," I said, uttering a big sigh. After finding all those coins we were still so blue and missing Pa.

We took note of the little tunnel that led to the small cave where the Bible was found. It had a low entrance, one not shown on the drawing. This was the tunnel in which we found the money, and we left the lantern in the small cut out in this tunnel. I was trying to find something that looked like it would be right under the tunnel. There was nothing to be found.

Were we missing a drawing?

Looking back at Dad studying Pa's Bible, my heart sank with compassion for him. My world would fall apart if I lost my Dad, and on top of that, not knowing what happened to him!

"Did you find something, Dad?"

"No, nothing unusual."

The rest of the evening, after our dinner, was spent relaxing. Mark was certainly on the mend and could open his mouth wide enough to eat small portions of food.

Dad took time to tend Mark with some new bandages and checked his nose too. He was doing very well. Mark said he hadn't even thought about his head wound and nose with all the excitement of the day.

Dad searched through the papers one more time to see where the scraping sound might be coming from.

He laid one map over the other and they seemed to match perfectly. He found one tunnel that looked like it ran right under the one we were in. He noticed it also ran to the gorge edge. Now how do we get there, to find it?

Our task for the next day was decided. The tunnel also seemed to lead in the direction of the coach house. That was going to be fun.

He decided we would go to the gorge and see if we could find another entrance into the rock wall, or anything else that would give us a clue. We knew we might face the cougar, so we would take matches and gunpowder.

Dad said, "If that cougar lives there, it must be possible for it to get around to hunt, raccoons, deer, or other small animals."

Dad told us that cats were at the top of their food chain and their actions were unpredictable. We should stay sharp and alert.

"They are most active at dusk and dawn so we will not go early, and hopefully not stay late." Dad added.

We needed a good night's sleep even though we were not as safe and secure as before. This changed how we felt about our hideaway. Before, there was no doubt it was the safest place and now, well, anything could happen. We would need to protect ourselves if someone else was down here. Dad put a large metal pry bar beside his bed. He found it behind the kitchen cabinet.

"Good night boys," came confidently from his lips as we relaxed and soon fell asleep.

CHAPTER 45

The Last Tunnel Before Our Find!

Breakfast was accompanied by outbursts of chatter as we tried to out-talk one another. Planning for today, talking about our coins, the cougar, what the gunpowder would do and so on, were all part of our conversation.

Dad finally calmed us down long enough to get packed.

We took everything that we thought would be useful. I emptied my pouch to clean it up and noticed I had spilled a little gunpowder in it. Turning it inside out and shaking it as well, I gave it a good brushing. I noticed there was something drawn on it! My pouch was leather and the drawing was done in ink. It looked like it was done in real ink, and not ballpoint.

"Hey, look what I found!"

We studied the map. "Pa gave me this bag, so he must have known about this! Right?"

It seemed to be the passage from the carriage house to the gorge, leading to the underground lake tunnel and then back up to the passage we knew and then to the storage room.

"That is almost a full circle, isn't it?" I questioned.

This would make life a lot easier, or so I thought.

Knowing that we couldn't see well in the tunnel, we took our time to study some more drawings and make certain we weren't missing anything.

As I was studying the sketch on my bag, I realized it also seemed to go off the edge of the gorge. We already knew the familiar tunnel led us to the edge of the rock wall, and now this one too?

"Do you see this? This tunnel coming from our carriage house goes right off over the gorge."

Dad had tried to lay two plans on top of one another and found the two openings to open air were very close together.

Dad said it was proof of what he suspected last night.

"Yes, I think this is a confirmation that we have to go and . . . maybe meet the cougar."

"Is everyone in?" Dad asked. We both gave a positive reply.

This time we took an extra lantern, fuel and food. My pouch was now a map and hung empty, inside out. All of its contents were carefully stored in the side pocket of my backpack. The climb down was getting easier as we were getting accustomed to the distance and knew what to expect. As we neared the bottom, Dad took the gunpowder and made a small trail along the whole distance of the large natural cavern and from the tunnel to the gorge.

He said, "Now if the cougar shows up, light the powder and that should scare it away."

We nodded in agreement.

"Do you both have matches?"

We nodded while standing outside trying not to look at the sun.

It was nice to see the daylight, but it almost hurt ours eyes. Squinting, we looked back towards the top of the gorge. We were so far down, and yet so far up from the river. There was a rock wall jutting out overhead forming a canopy. When you exited the cave, there was about 10 feet of a grassy ridge to walk on. It was very sloped, with many rocks dispersed here and there. If you watched your step and walked, it felt quite safe.

Beyond the grassy ledge, a long way down, lay the mighty Niagara. While looking down I recalled the night Mac and I found this place and how much more intriguing it was at night.

It also jarred my thoughts back to the cat! After taking a quick look around, we were satisfied. The three of us scanned the sides and studied them to see if there was anything that looked like a path. You could scale the rocks in a couple of areas, but nothing that we wanted to attempt.

Dad said the map looked like there were the two entrances which sat right one above the other. I looked at my pouch. I only saw one entrance go out to the gorge. *Why is it different?* My lines looped around back to the gazebo stairs.

Dad said he would tie a rope to a tree growing out of the rock and let himself down to look around. I told him I would go as he could pull me up if need be. We would have a harder time with him.

He chuckled. "So you think I need to lose weight, do you?"

"No." He cut me off and said he understood, but was going himself.

The rope was tightly tied to the tree. Dad put the other end around him and made a good strong knot.

"Now you boys put the rope around that boulder and let me down slowly."

I didn't like the way the rope tied into a knot. It was a thick rope and didn't seem tight enough.

We were nervous, but would hang on to it for dear life. We let the rope slide down slowly until Dad was out of sight. He told us to stop. We wrapped and tied the rope so we could have a look at him. Our heads were leaning over the edge to see if we could get a glimpse of him when to our surprise, he wasn't there.

"Dad," I called.

He replied, "Don't worry I'm okay. There is a tunnel down here."

"Can we come?"

"I am going to take a quick look around, you stay right there."

After a couple of minutes, we called again and got no response. We wondered if we should pull the rope up and go down ourselves. Minutes seemed like an eternity.

We froze as we heard a voice behind us.

"Boys, I am over here."

We turned to see Dad standing on a rock ledge! We made our way over and noticed a tall but narrow rift in the rock wall behind him. We had gathered the rope and left it near the face of the wall at the entrance. We climbed a few feet carrying all the gear to meet Dad. This was better than hanging over the cliff—that was for sure!

The rock stairway continued down to the tunnel below. We had our lanterns lit and one flashlight on, as we carefully followed the downward path. It was going to be a long hike again.

"We should look for clues regarding the scratching sound yesterday," exclaimed Mark.

We spotted an old rag and an old knife. That was an unexpected find. The stairs going down weren't long before the ground leveled out and it became very effortless as we moved ahead.

We were really having the time of our lives and enjoying each other in conversation. Mark was telling us what he would do if he saw the cat and we roared with laughter, forgetting why we were there.

Just as Dad was telling us to keep it down, a bright light shone directly at us. We were blinded and could see nothing but a huge ball of light.

We put our hands up to our eyes, to shield them.

Dad asked, "Who are you? Talk to us."

There was nothing but silence.

Eventually a weak, raspy though familiar voice came out of the darkness.

CHAPTER 46

The Greatest Treasure Found

Dad said who we were and the light went off. We instantly shone our lights to find the person.

He was standing there before us, derelict and emaciated.

We could tell his face was gaunt, even from under his matted long beard. The person looked shabby and his clothes were torn and soiled. He collapsed. We ran over to help him. Dad knelt over him as he studied the stranger's face.

Suddenly he recognized the face and started to shout, "Dad, Dad!"

It was Pa! We could hardly believe it. *Was he hiding down here?* My heart was pounding at the realization that Pa was alive and we had found him.

It looked like we were just in time. He looked ill.

"Let's lay him down in his room; it's the one in which we found his Bible, not too far from here. He has a sleeping bag and some food in there, as we saw earlier."

Pa was passed out and weighed so little that Dad carried him and we took the supplies. It was difficult getting him through the low narrow crevice in the rock beside the lake. We laid him on a blanket and pulled him through the low opening without hurting him.

Dad put him on his cot and covered him up.

"Can you two get some branches from outside, so I can make a fire?" he asked.

We took Dad's headband light, and another flashlight. Dad reminded us to take some gunpowder, so we did.

"Be careful boys!"

We nodded as we left. Dad stayed with Pa, trying to bring him around. He opened a can of soup to heat later. He hoped Pa would wake soon, as he stroked his grey matted hair so lovingly and spoke to him gently.

We were almost outside when we heard the cougar.

"Let's grab a few twigs and go."

We quickly grabbed what we could find and each had a small armful. We went back in the tunnel towards the underground lake. For some reason, we felt like we were being followed. It was an eerie feeling as if evil lurked around every corner. I grabbed the rag and knife we had stepped over earlier. We walked quickly, but did not run, ever mindful of our surroundings, and what Dad told us about cougars. We didn't have much longer to go, but knew the cougar was very close. Too close! We suddenly heard him behind us.

We both yelled in low and loud voices raising our hands and lights. As we looked back we saw the outline of the cougar.

"I think we scared it away with the noise and light."

"That was timely," Mark replied.

We kept on going.

Arriving at the small cave, we put the wood on the fire pit using the cloth for kindling. It was getting nice and warm so Dad took advantage of it and heated the can of chicken soup. We opened some crackers and cheese and apples we had brought with us. It was the best lunch while sitting there looking at my Pa, even though he was so ill. I knew he was going to be just fine.

My mind drifted back to our family prayers and how God answered, only to be interrupted by the thoughts of the cougar.

We told Dad that we had seen the cat, and shone the lights on it as we yelled. Thankfully it looked like it was scared away.

Pa was stirring and Dad went to talk to him.

"Are you alright?"

Pa tried to say yes, but just uttered a squeak.

"Don't talk," said Dad as he tried to feed him some soup. It was hot and would make him feel some warmth from the inside.

Dad spoke showing great concern: "When you can talk, we need to know the easiest way to get you out of here, Dad. I mean just to the hideout of course. I know that someone is looking to hurt us."

Pa nodded and mumbled, "Omz was killed by them. They wanted to kill you, so I disappeared."

He became teary-eyed and Dad put his strong arms around Pa and held him tightly. It didn't look like Pa had the strength to ever give anybody one of his bear hugs again. It made me sad to see him this way.

"We will talk later Dad. Try to get some sleep."

Pa closed his eyes in a most peaceful way and you could see he would rest well knowing we were there.

It seemed like hours until Pa wakened and opened his eyes again. He tried to sit up but lacked the strength. It was too much of an effort, and he was forced to lie back on his cot.

"Have you been down here for all these months?"

He nodded, while lifting his head from the pillow.

Dad told him we had found out about the tunnels and someone had tried to kill Bee. Pa just wept and covered his face with his skeleton-like hands. We told him Mom and Bee were safe and far away. We were trying to find out what this was all about so the girls could come back to a safe home.

Pa looked at Mark with a question on his brow.

Dad explained how Mark was badly beaten up by Vinnie and he was here for his own protection. No one knew where he was, or if he was even alive. The police had probably been notified by now. Mark's mom, who would be a complete basket case by now, was a concern that we had no answer for right now.

Pa looked a little more relaxed again. He said Vinnie was the one who had hired someone to kill Omz. We were so startled at that fact that it left us all speechless. Finally, after a long silence, Dad helped Pa sit and gave him some warm water to drink to soothe his throat.

There were no words to describe what we felt.

"I feel better now," Pa whispered in a weak voice.

"Vinnie is the great-grandson of a man who worked these tunnels in the days of your Grandfather, and Josh, your Great-Opa. Somehow the worker got word out of some great conspiracy to his family, and about the money that was to be hidden on this property. He never said anything about the tunnels or the kind of work he was doing. This I found out in my investigations.

"Vinnie came here to find some gold and get rich at any cost. The story had been ingrained in his mind ever since he was a child and Vinnie was going to be the one to find it. His family continuously told stories of the gold they would find in Canada if they only could get there. Every time a story was told it grew and the amount of gold multiplied. Apparently, this worker never got out of here and neither did any of the others."

Dad told him of the papers he read that stated the workers should all be killed.

"Dad can you tell us how to get to the top from here?"

He nodded.

"Do you think with my help you can make it?"

Pa nodded yes.

I said, "What about the cougar, Dad?"

"He won't hurt you as long as you are with me." Pa whispered strongly, ending in a loud choking cough that lasted for minutes.

We thought he must still be delirious, as cougars are wild animals and wouldn't hesitate to kill us!

Suddenly we heard a loud growl.

"Get behind me boys," came the strained order from Pa.

We did as he said in hopes that he knew what he was doing.

Dad joined us, ready to throw his lantern at the animal.

Pa pleaded, "Please don't hurt him, he is my only friend down here. He saved my life many times."

The cougar cautiously started his approach towards Pa; he didn't trust the new visitors yet. With a slow calculated prowl, he moved across the cave floor. When he got close enough he licked Pa's face and Pa reached out his hand to pet him. Pa let him know he was fine and we were his friends. He moved close enough to sniff us, to get our scent. As if he knew and understood Pa's words, he looked up at us again.

"Now you go and guard the place, I am well," commanded Pa.

The cougar licked him once more and turned to leave.

He looked back, as if to say, *Are you sure?* And Pa said, "Go on."

The cougar left slowly.

"He won't hurt you now. He has your scent and knows you are with me, now he is your friend and will protect you."

We came out of our shock one by one and were still in disbelief of what we had just witnessed.

Dad asked Pa if he was ready and we got our things together. We put the fire out and took another look around. We left through the tunnel, as Pa directed. Dad asked Pa what the scratching or scraping sound was yesterday when we were down here. The noise came from somewhere below us. Pa said he didn't know except that he had passed out in the tunnel and when he came to, the cougar was scratching the rock over and over as if to wake him. The tunnel above had a very small cave and concealed it well although it let sound easily travel through it. He could hear if someone was down here in either tunnel.

"Hey is that where we found the chest with the coins?" I blurted out.

Pa was surprised we had found it and said, "Yes that's the one."

"We didn't see a hole, did we?" Mark added.

Dad said, no, we were looking down and only at the chest, and forgot to look around.

From Pa's hide-away cave we had to make our way back to the other tunnel, as it led to the carriage house. Pa said it was the easiest route back.

Pa went through the lower tunnel escorted every step of the way. He was supported totally by Dad. We were directed to the far side of another dried up underground lake.

Apparently the men had orders to drain it years ago, before any of us, before even Pa, knew about this place. Pa told us it was in one of the letters he found. They used it to put in a lot of the rock rubble from the constructing of the tunnels.

On the other side, tucked behind a jutting boulder, was another opening! You had to know where it was to find it.

CHAPTER 47

The Tunnel to the Carriage House

Pa was tired and we sat him down for a while.

"Is there another way back to our storage room from here?" Dad asked.

Pa said, "No, this passage was used just by the workers to get down into the shafts never to return. They didn't even know about the supplies and the tunnels connecting to them. They used different crews to do separate jobs.

"They had sacks over their heads when taken from one area to another. I will show you."

We were on our way again and Dad climbed step after step, then Pa said, "Stop."

There was a human-sized opening in the wall. It was a deep crevice, and the inside looked like it dropped indefinitely. Our lights couldn't reach the bottom.

"All I know is that the workers were told to climb down on a rope to the bottom and start a new cave. The ropes were extremely long and there were many of them. They had a narrow but long platform built to hold the ropes and men so that they could use it to go up or down. When all the men were on the ropes and descending they were set on fire from the top. They all fell to their deaths. You can see for yourself. The sacks, which the men were permitted to remove for the climb, are still lying there." It gave us the chills. We were standing at the edge of this, a diabolic tomb.

"This, my father told to me," Pa said with great sadness.

"The German owner of the house confided in him before he went back to Germany. He wanted to appease his conscience, as it bothered him so much. He said he would have been killed along with his family if he didn't follow orders. He also said that he was ordered to destroy the tunnels with gunpowder, but the German landlord loved them and could not go through with the order."

Pa said that his Dad, my Great-Opa Wittfoot, told him all of this but never went down here. He left everything as it was, respecting the graves of the men who died here.

"My dad was the one who left it all the same and I was the one who changed the house to have hidden escapes to the tunnels below. "

He said, "While I remodeled the Carriage House, I kept the connection to the tunnels. I discretely remodeled that entrance myself. Your Great-Opa's stories intrigued me so much that I did all this in private. Even the graveyard was my idea."

"That is the worst death trap." I almost shouted.

"Yes, it is meant to be," said Pa.

"Did you straighten the tap out?" He questioned me intently.

"Yes I did!"

"Well that makes the water flow through the tunnel with great force," Pa replied.

"Well I almost got killed going over the gorge," I declared.

I told him how I avoided it with great difficulty, and he was very impressed as well as thankful that I had survived.

"That was for snoopers," he said.

We all thought that radical, but had to remind ourselves that someone had been trying to kill Bee and had succeeded in killing Omz.

Pa added, "It was a direct line to the main cave and once in the tunnel it couldn't be missed. Before I redesigned the tunnel it only contained a water trickle."

Pa said he got a note from someone in Germany saying he wanted the money and the secret or he would kill the family. This was a couple of years before Omz's accident and he said that he did not think they were serious.

"I just ignored it, but never told you both anything about this place. I figured the less you knew the safer you would be.

"When Omz died, then I too, took it seriously. Afterwards I blamed myself for ignoring the warning. I felt so responsible and wanted to keep my family safe."

He couldn't bear losing another family member because of money. He had no idea where the money was, at that time.

"That is why you didn't tell me about all of this."

"That's right."

"Of course I couldn't resist, telling the boy pieces of what sounded like nonsense, but they were total reality. I needed to leave information if something happened to me."

He looked at me as he spoke.

"Well, let's keep going. We need to put you to bed for a rest, Dad."

We couldn't forget the horror story we had just been told and tried not to think of those poor men.

The stairs became steep and we had to stop many times.

I told Pa it reminded me of when Mac and I were down in the other tunnel, and she got a concussion. The cougar came after us and we hid in a cave.

Pa said that he remembered someone screaming in a high-pitched voice.

He thought they had found him out and were coming to kill him. He had been feeling very poorly for weeks and couldn't move too quickly, so he moved to the lower room, without much provision. Since his illness began he had lost a lot of weight.

We were glad we found Pa or he found us. It was nice being together. Pa started coughing hard. He said he had this cold for a long time. I gave him a sweet candy from my backpack.

"Thanks, you seem to have everything in there. Do you still have my pouch?" he asked in between coughs.

"Yep that is what helped us find you."

"Well, you are a clever one."

—~—

The stop-and-go seemed like hours but it was acceptable for the company we had retrieved. We were now relaxed and had nothing pushing us. It was a good time talking and catching up with life as we slowly advanced. Pa thought we should be near the top soon.

"Over there!" he shouted. "Make sure no one sees you."

We let him reach for the door and he pulled out a piece of wood and turned it.

I jumped back. "This isn't a slide, is it?"

From under his over-grown beard we were met with a weary ear-to-ear grin, knowing very well what I was referring to.

"No, this is different."

Dad took over as Pa tried to pull the wall downward. He was too weak to get the job done. We watched as it disappeared in the floor.

"Nice," said Mark.

We came out and walked up into the garage. The door closed automatically. He showed us how to open it from the garage.

Just then we heard a noise outside. We heard voices shouting in anger with the foulest language. Opening the secret door again we entered the tunnel and closed it. No one could know about this place.

"Okay." I said, adding, "But we can't see what is going on from here. You stay here with Pa and I will go back and up the other way."

"It shouldn't take too long, right? The cougar is our friend, right . . . Pa?"

CHAPTER 48

Caught

Pa said the cougar would not hurt us now.

Mark and I took our light as Dad and Pa sat on the stairs waiting for our okay.

Pa was weak and shivering from cold as his body was cooling after all that climbing, even though Dad almost carried him. We were so close to warmth, and yet they had to stay hidden in the cold. Mark and I both gave Dad our jackets to put over Pa. We would be warm running down and then up the stairs.

We made good time with my headband light and another flashlight. We also left our backpacks behind. We moved much quicker than I would have ever thought we could. In 25 minutes, we had reached the bottom and were past the lake and back into the familiar tunnel.

We made our way through the cougar cavern being careful not to slip. We were going to enter the stairs going up when we heard men running and yelling.

"We've got you now, you will never escape."

We quickly turned our lights off and headed back to the crossroads. The voices would probably go to the light and outside so we hid just inside the tunnel going the opposite way, where it was dark.

As a man ran by we could make out the voice of Vinnie yelling and shouting vulgarities. He headed right to the where the light was coming in, through the opening of the gorge wall. Running at top speed while slipping, he was as out of control and it looked like nothing would stop him.

He ran at full speed into the open air of the small ridge. We couldn't tell if he was trying to stop, as our view was minimal. All we heard was a diminishing yell as he dropped hundreds of feet to the bottom.

We were upset with hearing his death cry and in shock, but we were snapped back to reality. There was another voice. There was someone else.

I didn't recognize the voice as he called for Vinnie, but I recognized that smell. He was the guy who followed us from the hospital. He yelled and we hoped that he would go towards the edge of the gorge and not come in our direction.

If we could hit him over the head with something we could get a lot of questions answered.

"Vinnie!" he yelled in a high-pitched whiney voice. "Where are you?"

We were as quiet as church mice, trying not to breathe. He just stood at the crossroads for a second. He noticed the light coming from the opening in the opposite direction from us. *Good.* He went through the tunnel, but not fast enough.

He was cautious, walked carefully and took notice of what was around him. Then he took out a cigarette and lit it. He threw the match back, over his shoulders, and it hit the ground.

We remembered the gunpowder trail. It also led in our way, and we scrambled to take refuge in the little cave, not far from here. It made a blaze of fire, both ways, and the man went running out of the tunnel.

"Vinnie!" he called, when suddenly out of nowhere came the cougar.

He hugged the wall as if trying to become one with it. The cougar growled at him and exposed his claws to his face. The man fell to the ground in fear and lay there with his face covered, crying with a high pitch, which irritated the big cat even more.

The cougar closed in on him, clawed at his back and shredded his very expensive suit.

The gunpowder had all burned up and we came out from our safe dark hideaway. It was so smoky that we had to feel our way along the rock wall of the tunnel with our tee shirts over our mouths. *What was going on out there?* We could hear strange sounds.

We could not believe our eyes.

The growling cougar was standing on top of the man, keeping his face and body tight to the ground. It was our chance; we got the rope that we had used to let Dad down.

We tied him up so he could just barely walk and his hands were tied as tightly as possible. The rope was awkward to use, as it was so large and heavy.

We told the cougar to watch him and not let him go, or, he could eat him.

The next step was to take him to the little shelter where Mac and I stayed and we told him to push the rock in front of the opening, and the cougar couldn't kill him.

Mark and I left the cougar to guard our captive and were off to see how they got in our secret hideaway. He seemed scared enough not to move and we knew the cougar would not let him out. We heard yelling as we walked away.

"Please don't leave me, please don't leave me here!"

CHAPTER 49

Who Else Knew Our Secret?

Climbing the stairs felt effortless. Our adrenaline was pumping and we were on a mission. Dad and Pa would be wondering what happened to us.

We were nearing the secret door to our storage room, and I noticed the light was on.

"Hey, who found out about the light? Let's check the storage room and make sure there is no one in there."

We opened the door and went in.

"No, no one here," I mumbled. The door closed behind us, we went down the rock hallway towards our living room. We opened our living quarters trap door and climbed out. It was nice to be back.

Mark pointed and said, "Look!" as quietly as possible.

There on the bed, all covered up with a sleeping bag, was the body of a person.

Wondering, who in the world would be in our bed, I grabbed something hard. It was a frying pan. I gave Mark the crowbar and snuck up to the lump on the bed. I pulled the sleeping bag off suddenly and Mark was ready to clobber the person.

It was Mac! I recognized the streaks of glow in the dark spray she used in her hair at times.

"Stop! Don't hit her!" I yelled.

We got out our light, as she was not moving. *Oh no, what hap-*

pened to her?

There was no blood anywhere, so we called, "Mac ... Mac!"

She stirred, "Where am I? Is Vinnie here?"

We said he was dead and she was safe.

After a lot of prodding and work, we got her to sit up and tell us what she was doing here. She seemed to be so groggy and slurred her words.

Vinnie and another guy kidnapped her. The other man drugged her, and put her in the back of their car. They had tried to get information out of her with threats, but she wouldn't break.

"They left me helpless and drugged in the back seat. When I came to and saw the gazebo in the distance, I started for it. I was still feeling so drunk and forgot to close the car door."

When Vinnie came from around the carriage house with his partner, I heard him say, "Hey, who opened the car door?"

"I didn't know how far behind me they were so I just kept on struggling forward. It was like being in a dream when you can't run but you need to."

One yelled, "There she is, let's get her."

"I crawled in under the gazebo and put the light on. I was just so disoriented that I could not see where I was going. Down the stairs I stumbled hoping to make it. My thought was to get the doors closed before they got down here. If I succeeded, they wouldn't know how to open the door to this room. I covered myself up and passed out. I hoped the doors were closed. Were the doors both closed?

"Hope I didn't give your secret away, Josh," she whimpered.

"No, no, don't worry, it turned out okay. We will tell you about all the details later."

"Mark can you stay here with Mac and I will get Dad and Pa?"

"You got it," replied Mark.

As I left to go up to the study, so I could be more inconspicuous, I heard Mac questioning, "Did he say 'Pa', or am I still dreaming?"

I hurried up the stairs and into the study then got into my childhood hiding spot and went through the wall into the parlor with the French doors. It looked very quiet out there.

The car was parked in the driveway near the coach house and the back door was still wide open. Mac must have been terrified. They probably wanted to start at the coach house and we would have been caught. *That was close.*

I went into the garage, closing the door behind me and opened the door to where Dad and Pa were. Dad was holding Pa and trying to keep him warm. They were glad to see me.

"Okay we can go to the mansion now and to our safe place. Wait till you hear what happened!"

"I knew something was up, it took you forever."

"You were right Dad. Never mind the car outside, everything is good."

We slowly and cautiously made our way to the mansion as not to be seen, almost carrying Pa. He was getting so weak. As we entered the secret hall Dad suggested we use the slide. He said he would put Pa on his legs and on his lap and buffer his stop. I told him I would go first and put down the pillow and sleeping bag. He agreed.

I went first and did as was suggested. Before I knew it Dad came down and I braced him at the bottom. We made it and went next door. We would put Pa into a nice warm bed.

The heater was on and Dad made Pa and Mac a cup of chicken soup. Pa closed his eyes after a few spoonfuls and drifted off. Mac on the other hand was getting very alert and wanted to know everything. She seemed to be getting more hyper by the second, and it was difficult to keep her quiet.

We filled them in on what happened to Vinnie and where his partner in crime was. Mac got terrified at the thought of the killer still being so near. We assured her that she was safe here with us and there was no need to fear anything.

Dad and I decided to go and check on the suit guy, while Mark took care of Pa and Mac. Dad and I went down the stairs and turned the corner to the little shelter where he was a prisoner. We were shocked to find the rock moved and the rope lying inside.

"Oh, no, do you think Mac is in danger?" I blurted out.

Dad said, "Let's not jump to conclusions."

We went back towards the, what was now, quickly fading daylight. There was the cougar.

"He would never let him get away, Dad."

Looking around we noticed a designer shoe at the edge of the cliff. We walked over and peered into the gorge.

"I think that is him way over there. He must have fallen. He can't be alive after dropping that distance." Dad just stood gazing down.

I praised the cougar, "Good boy." I kicked the shoe off the cliff.

Getting back to tell the others of our find was a delightful task. We finally felt free again.

We would send Mac back home. She seemed to be safe now and settled down to her normal self. She could find out if anyone else was involved. Her Dad would have information and could keep her safe if needed.

Vinnie had kidnapped her this morning when she was checking the graveyard to see if there was a note. They were snooping around when she came by. They gagged her, and then dragged her to the car where they drugged her, after hours of questioning.

She had no bruises and wasn't hurt. Her parents would just think she was out for the day, so she could go back without causing suspicion. We had to keep our secret for now. We needed to have time to talk about all the things we had learned and what Pa found out on those trips abroad. It was getting late and Mac would have to leave soon.

Mark, on the other hand, had been gone for a longer time and would have to have a good story. We decided the truth was the best story, but that he was hiding out in the mansion. Vinnie, and his accomplice, would come after him, slip over the gorge and fall to their deaths. With that story Mark could also have left, except for his stitches.

They were not ready to come out yet and he would have to stay a while longer. His face was still shades of green, yellow and bluish bruises. His gash was still not totally healed when we unwound the bandage.

The decision was made to let no one know about the secrets of the mansion or the tunnels under it, never mind the unfortunate deaths of all those tunnel builders.

There were still so many unanswered questions. What did I trip over in the tunnel from the graveyard tunnel? Was there more treasure hidden in these caves? How much was the treasure we found worth?

Pa said, “He hid more papers with more tunnel drawings.”

Where would they lead? Did anyone else know of our secrets? What were we going to do with the money chest? Dad said time would tell and we would figure it all out.

We nursed Pa back to health and it didn’t take long before he started regaining his strength. All he needed was some medication for his cold, good nourishing food, rest and above all, those who loved him.

Mark was nicely healed within a few more days and Dad removed the stitches. He was ready to go home. His mother would be shocked at the sight of him and I could just imagine all the hugs and kisses that she would smother him with. Mark didn’t want to leave except to see his mom. His absence had caused her a lot of pain. She would be so overwhelmed with joy at his reappearance.

We told him when we were back from holidays that we would include him in some of our adventure. He was thrilled and hugged everyone good-bye. He and Dad had formed a special bond and I could tell he regarded and loved him like a father. Dad had been so kind and compassionate with him and they talked for hours about Mark’s life.

Pa filled us in on so many aspects of his life both down here and in the real world. We wished he could have confided in us sooner.

He had been trying to find the names and families of all the men who were murdered for the secrets of this property. He wanted to honour their ancestors’ lives and repay them in a small way.

Pa had information on most of their ancestors. He just had to locate them in the various countries to where they immigrated.

“Pa, wasn’t Vinnie one of them?” I asked a little worried. “What if there are more like him?”

“Well, I wanted to do it all anonymously.”

We decided that was good and we would work on that later.

We had to come up for a story regarding Pa’s return. He would have to come back from his travels from a far off very remote place.

He was extremely ill and couldn't get word out because of his poor condition. He certainly looked the part. His ID was stolen and they didn't have a number to call at the distant outpost. When well enough, he made his way back home after applying for a new passport.

Dad and I would meet, and then return with Mom and Bee, our bikes on the rack, just as we left. We would stay hidden until then.

Mac and Mark visited, but not too often as they did not want to tip off anyone about the hiding spot.

Barry, Mac's dad, had found out that Vinnie hired the suit guy to help him find some kind of treasure. Vinnie had been in the area long before he acknowledged he was Mark's long lost relative.

Vinnie had a water delivery business. He owned his own water delivery truck, which had a power hose attached. Vinnie's country of origin was Germany and that made a lot of sense. Pa was so saddened by the thought of Vinnie killing his beloved wife. Now there was more proof that he had done it.

CHAPTER 50

Mark Re-Appears

Mark's mom was so overwhelmed at the sight of her son that she fell to her knees and sobbed bitterly. After Mark's hugs and comfort, it finally sank in that he was alive and back. Her happiness could not be expressed.

He told her about Vinnie and his almost deadly beating and how Vinnie and his friend fell over the gorge chasing him. His mom was so upset with the beating he endured at the hands of Vinnie.

She had no idea, and was immensely disturbed by it. Mark assured her that he was all right and for her not to worry. Because of Vinnie she had sent to Germany for papers regarding her ancestry. She hoped he was not one of her relatives and intended on kicking him out of her home.

They called Barry, and Mark told him all the details he knew. When Barry came for a statement he said he wasn't surprised with what he had uncovered about Vinnie.

Barry had come by the house and found the car with the back door wide open. He looked around but didn't find anything else. Mark's story made sense and they sent a recovery team, to retrieve the bodies.

The paper played up the part of the suit being torn to shreds by what looked like cougar claws. Everyone in the area was hit with paranoia and wouldn't hang out near the gorge. This was good for all our sakes.

CHAPTER 51

Pa's Return

Pa went to stay at the mansion. Of course, we were not "home" yet from our pretend family trip. He pretended not to know where we were, and asked Barry if he knew. Barry delighted to see him, listened to his story and shook his head.

"Do you know how worried your family was? They thought you might be dead! They were in such anguish over your disappearance!"

Pa of course did and hoped we would be home soon.

Mark and Mac visited him often and made sure he was fine. Mark's mom made some meals for him and he loved that good, old fashioned, home cooking.

We arrived four days later, as Bee and Mom needed time to arrange a ride back and pick up their car where we met them.

CHAPTER 52

Saying Good-Bye

Mom had been at the hospital with Grammy a couple of times. Grammy was going to be fine but had developed diabetes. She didn't feel well so stopped eating because of this.

The doctors explained to her how important it was to eat regularly and in small amounts. She was trained and educated as to what she should eat and the portion sizes. The hardest part was to learn to give herself the injections. Grammpy also learned how to do this in case the need arose.

We were so grateful that she was going to be fine. We had just gotten over all the medical issues when we got a call to arrange a ride home and that all was well. Mom was so excited and Bee ... not so much.

She loved to see her family together again, but she loved being with Kelly. She was saddened by the thought of not seeing him anymore. They had become good friends and Kelly had shown her the highest measure of respect, not even giving her one kiss.

Kelly was invited down the night before they left and Grammy made a wonderful meal for everyone to enjoy. Normally they would go to church with Grammy and Grammpy the next day. In the past their experience found it to be an old-fashioned Mennonite Church. Many came with horse and buggy and others with vehicles. They could arrive in whichever manner they chose instead of being told to follow a human-made rule. Bee and Mom liked this and felt quite at home in this church. They knew they could wear their hair in any fashion or dress as they wished and still be accepted. This was difficult for Mom to grasp at first as she took such ridicule as a child from the Amish community. The congregation had an acceptance of people for who they were in the eyes of God, and not what they looked like.

Kelly wanted to come by early in the morning to see them off and Bee thought that was so nice of him. It was morning, their driver was punctual as usual and they had their, "city clothes" on. Kelly had never seen Bee in her modern attire before and couldn't stop looking at her. She looked even more beautiful than before.

They were about to get into the vehicle and Mom was hugging Grammy and Grammpy as Bee already had. It took Bee completely by surprise when Kelly put his arms around her and quickly kissed her. She was stunned and blushed a little.

Kelly whispered, "I asked your mum if that was okay."

"Oh, okay," said Bee, not knowing what to say next.

They had already exchanged email addresses and as well as phone numbers and snail mail addresses. They would communicate in one of those ways. Everyone was waving as they lost sight of one another. It was going to be a quiet ride home.

CHAPTER 53

The Homecoming

It was so good to see both Bee and Mom. Bee seemed to have grown up even more, and said she had made friends and had an awesome time in Amish country. Before they left she had been miserable because she thought she would be bored in Amish country. What happened?

"Wait until you get home and see what we have for you there!" I exclaimed.

"What?" Bee pleaded.

"Wait and see."

It was the longest ride home, as I tried to keep my mouth shut, and not give our secret away.

We drove onto the yard and right up to the mansion.

"This is where we will live from now on," Dad said with a big grin.

"No, Dad, this is Pa's house, isn't he coming back?" Bee cried out eyes tearing.

"Pa said we could live here with him."

Just then Pa stepped out onto the wide porch after coming through the French doors.

All car doors swung open at one time and Mom and Bee made a dash to embrace Pa.

It was nice to stand back and just take in the sight of my family, all together again. We would live together, all in one house. I couldn't wait to get started.

Pa and I could walk around once more and I could listen to his stories, but this time I knew they were true. We had so many tunnels to discover and equally as many mysteries waiting to be revealed. How much money was hidden, and how much gold could there have been? It would all have to wait until another time.

For now we would enjoy being together with people we loved and concentrate on what really mattered in life—our greatest treasure—our family!

Acknowledgements

This book is the result of a long-hidden dream. Having had problems writing my letters and numbers in proper sequence since childhood, it seemed impossible. I would read books, billboards, etc., three times so that I could make out the words and would continuously write my numbers backwards.

In high school, my class library teacher noticed my diligent, yet snail's pace at reading. He showed me how to read with a bookmarker under each line and look at a group of words, instead of each word individually. I tried this and with practice it revolutionized my reading. I got through many library books, and from then on enjoyed reading and even practiced reading out loud.

I give an appreciative thank you to all teachers who inspire their students, especially the ones with learning disabilities.

There are countless seeds strewn in classrooms that a teacher might never see grow. Be assured they will develop, and the students will make a difference in the world because of them.

These days there is an abundance of aid to assist making learning a wonderful experience, but nothing compares to the support and encouragement of that authority figure, the teacher or parent. I praise those parents who work diligently, never tiring, in struggling to help their children. They make learning a powerful and exciting experience.

It did not take me long to write this book, and to this end, I thank two of my friends, Hazel, Sue and my daughter-in-law Nerissa, for their work to refine my grammar and make so many spelling corrections. They encouraged me to continue.

A big thank you also goes to my husband and best friend of 53 years. He patiently sat by as I struggled to spell correctly and write coherent sentences. Having an idea is one thing, but getting it down on paper is totally another.

I thank Josh for letting me use his name and those of some of his family and his friends.

About the Author

Margarete Ledwez was born in Germany, emigrating to Canada with her parents and brother when she was just a year old. She quickly developed a longing to create, which has eventually manifested itself in her writing.

Growing up in St. Catharines, Ontario, she became fascinated by the tunnels that had been used to hide slaves as part of the Underground Railroad and later by bootleggers during Prohibition.

While she and her husband were raising their own children they lived in Niagara Falls, just 5 kilometers from the celebrated "Screaming Tunnel." Her curiosity was once again piqued when she discovered the myths and legends surrounding the many tunnels under the famous falls, and when writing "Past Secret Present Danger," she drew from her knowledge as well as her unending intrigue that there could be many more tunnels yet to be discovered.

"Past Secret Present Danger" is Margarete Ledwez's first novel and the fulfillment of a long held dream; a story that has been evolving in the author's imagination for many years.

Margarete Ledwez lives in St. Catharines, Ontario with her husband, Harry.

CPSIA information can be obtained
at www.ICGtesting.com
Printed in the USA
LVOW03s1540210318
570659LV00002B/430/P